CARNIVAL
GYPSY

DOROTHY GILMAN BUTTERS

I0612160

Cover Design: Jolene MacFadden

Co-Contributor: Jonathan Butters

Co-Contributor: Christopher Butters

ISBN eBook (ePub) 978-1-961386-02-0

ISBN paperback 978-1-961386-03-7

ISBN hardback 978-1-961386-04-4

ISBN audio 978-1-961386-05-1

Originally Published by Grosset & Dunlap, Publisher, New York, 1950 – Starlight Novels Series

Table of Contents

[2nd] Edition - 2023
Published by
Southern Dragon Publishing
PO BOX 1712
Mayo, FL 32066
https://SouthernDragonPublishing.com
Author's Fansite: https://mrspollifax.com

INTRODUCTION AND NOTES BY

Dr. Jonathan W Butters is a Clinical Psychologist whose practice has consisted of treating adults with mood and personality disorders. He lives in Westchester County, NY and is Dorothy Gilman Butters' youngest son.

Christopher Butters is a retired court reporter after 30 years in the NYC court system, and a former union officer. He is also a poet. He is Dorothy Gilman Butters' oldest son.

Dear Reader:

This work of fiction was the second book published by Dorothy Gilman Butters. Originally published in 1950. There is a note in the beginning of the book, *"A condensation of this story appeared in SENIOR PROM"*. It can now be considered historical fiction. But there is some debate about that.

The storyline follows a young woman and her mother who inherit a Carnival that even includes a gypsy fortune-teller. There is a unique cast of characters and a well-told story that you will enjoy. We hope you will read this and the stories that follow with an open heart and mind.

CHAPTER ONE

Capri Maccomb sat upright on the old stuff sofa which was not so stuffed now that its springs were sagging and its tatters yielding up hands full of sawdust and horse hair. Her eyes matched the stillness of the room; the spring sun had darkened her fair skin and frivolously brightened her hair until she was all over tawny shade, like a gypsy. She sat with their hands and feet tidily crossed, anxious to make no sounds that might disturb the settling of their future. On Mr. Callandar's lips their future sounded a dismal, infinitely small thing. Capri supposed this meant they were penniless.

Across the room her mother, Francia, had perched on Uncle Shoe's traveling trunk and was watching the lawyer with kind eyes.

"Well," she said at last, "there's no postponing a bit of bad news, is there? We won't bite, you know."

Mr. Callandar sighed. He removed his glasses, blue on them and polished each lens with his handkerchief.

"You are quite prepared to hear the will?"

Francia leaned forward and smiled at him. Even in the dim twilight of the room she was beautiful, not as beautiful as in the pictures that covered one wall of the room, but still crisp-featured and slim despite the Gray threading her hair.

"We're prepared." The corners of her mouth turned down wryly. "Aren't we, darling?"

Capri nodded.

"Very well." The crackly sheets of paper were unfolded, Mr. Callandar's spectacles returned to their proper place, and in a dry, passionless voice he began reading "I, Schumann Abbott, being of sound mind and body..."

Capri's gaze wandered to the picture-lined walls, to the souvenirs of which Uncle Shoe had been so proud. There were smiling faces of people with whom he, and later Francia, had shared headlines and spotlights. She knew the autographs by heart; 'Always Yours, W.C. Fields'; 'Best of luck, Bill Robinson'; 'All Best Wishes, Darlings, Nora Bayes'. They were all there; Marie Dressler, Sophie Tucker, Weber and Fields, and a young man with a rope named Will Rogers. And there, too, was Uncle Shoe in caricature, photograph and drawing from the age of fourteen, when he trod the boards alone, to the later years when he and Francia, together had swept this country and Europe with their brother and sister act. King of all vaudeville they had called Uncle Shoe when he retired at last to the farm. Then vaudeville died, and now Uncle Shoe was dead, too, with only a few scratchy phonograph records and a trunk full of scrapbooks to remember him by.

And we're broke and it's not a bit surprising, thought Capri, remembering the hilarious failures they'd had in farming, the nights when Fran and Uncle Shoe had turned their backs on the diminishing bank accounts and pounded out old songs and minstrel stalls on the battered piano until the house had barely survived the noise and the shouting.

Mr. Callandar paused. Francia said, with a catch in her voice, "Well? And what are all Shoe's earthly possessions?"

Mr. Callandar cleared his throat. "This house," he said, removing his glasses once again and pointing them with distaste at the big shabby room.

"Mortgaged," said Francia.

"The twenty acres of land on which it stands."

"Full of rocks and perfectly terrible soil"

"The furnishings in the house."

"Worthless," said Francia, trying to smile.

"And the carnival."

"What?" gasped Francia.

Mr. Callandar nodded. "An atrocity called The Toby Brothers Traveling Show."

There was a terrifying silence. Then Francia stamped her foot. "Of all things!"

Capri laughed because this was so like Uncle Shoe. "You mean we own a carnival, Fran?"

Her mother nodded. "It would seem so." She threw up her hands helplessly. "When did this happen? Why did he never tell us he owned a carnival?"

Mr. Callandar winced. "For the same reason he did not consult me about it until it had been purchased-—the whole thing was a mistake. He bought it nearly fifteen years ago, and

3

has never received a penny from it. But he refused to sell. He said—-" Here Mr. Callandar coughed, "He said it gave him a bang to dabble in some kind of show business."

"Carnivals aren't show business," said Francia.

"I wouldn't know," replied Mr. Callandar coldly. "It was extremely foolish of him to buy it."

Francia leaned forward. "It's a flop, of course? The carnival, I mean. Like the farm?"

Mr. Callandar glanced through other papers. "It's worth scarcely a nickel," he said apologetically. "Of course I'm not surprised. Your brother, Mrs. Maccomb, was most adept at picking losers. The carnival is, uh, definitely third rate. The police seemed to raid it rather often, and I understand it is not allowed in any really respectable city. Games of chance, you know. Wheels of fortune."

Francia nodded, quite as though this were to be expected, and continued to study the floor.

Capri said brightly, "Well, anyway, we have a roof over our heads."

Her mother gave her a severe look. "Not just a roof, darling, a farm which takes money to run." She shrugged helplessly. "I did want to send you to college." At Mr. Callandar's interested glance, she added vaguely, "She gets rather good marks, you know."

Capri, who was at the moment far more interested in becoming an explorer, a nurse, or a poet, said nothing. This was her mother's scene and Capri was of necessity only a spectator.

"Shall I put the carnival up for sale, then?" asked Mr. Callandar. "I've taken the liberty of making out the necessary papers for you to sign."

Capri's mother sighed as she reached for the pen. "No one will ever buy it," she said.

"Oh, but on the contrary," said Mr. Callandar surprisingly, "there is someone who wants very much to buy it."

Francia paused, "Really?"

"Yes. It has been managed for many years by Mr.—-" He again consulted his papers. "By a Mr. Nicholas Sabo. Your brother had several offers from him, and upon hearing of your brother's death I received a telegram from him. I said it was worth scarcely a nickel, but he is willing to pay a very fair price. Yes, indeed, a very fair price."

Francia laid down the pin and frowned. "Why?" she asked simply. "Why should he want to buy it? You say my brother never received a profit from the carnival, and yet the one man who knows this wants to purchase it. Why?"

Mr. Callandar shrugged. "I have no idea."

Capri watched her mother stand up and walk absently over to the window. "How many rides does the carnival have?" she asked suddenly.

"I beg your pardon?"

"Rides. You know, loop-the-loops, merry-go-rounds. The size of every carnival is determined by the number of rides it owns. The sideshows are hired."

"Oh!" Mr. Callandar retreated to his papers and at last, victoriously, announced there were eight rides. A little flicker of curiosity moved across his face. "Is that large?" he inquired, in spite of himself.

Francia shook her head. "Small. Very small." She stared thoughtfully out the window. And Capri, waiting, knew that she looked out on rocky fields and unfertile slopes, a forlorn, run-down old mansion. As Mr. Callandar had said, Uncle Shoe was adept at picking losers.

Francia was thinking this, too. Aloud she said ruefully, "One old farm, good for nothing. One carnival, the same. Well, Capri, if you had to choose between the two, which would you take?"

Capri grinned. "The carnival, of course." She was not quite serious; by choosing the more incongruous she meant only that she was ready for anything. But her mother nodded.

"We can't keep both. We'll be lucky if we can hang onto one." She turned and faced Mr. Callandar resolutely. "Mr. Callandar," she said, "there's no use keeping the farm. Capri and I could never run it alone, and there's no money for help. We'll keep the carnival."

It brought Mr. Callandar to his feet with an exclamation. "But, my dear lady!" he cried in horror.

Francia whirled to face him. "Yes, yes," she cried. "Go ahead and say I'm mad. But we haven't a dime. I'm too old to sing and dance again; no one remembers me. This farm -—its bad years have ruined us. Yet here is a carnival that belongs to us and someone wants to buy it. Does anyone want to buy our farm? No. Therefore, there must be some hope for the carnival. Mustn't there, Mr. Callandar?"

"Well, really," stammered their lawyer, visibly overcome.

"What can I lose?" said Francia more calmly. "To me it is worth the chance. There is always the possibility that a carnival can be brought to life again. In a way, Mr. Callandar, that's my world."

"But your child!"

Capri started. Her mother threw her an amused glance. "Not exactly a child, Mr. Callandar. She can run a tractor and milk a cow. Can you milk a cow, Mr. Callandar?"

Their lawyer stiffened. "That's all right," said Francia. "Capri, you don't mind?"

Capri laughed. She laughed because Mr. Callandar's face looked like crumpled paper, and because there was enough of Uncle Shoe's blood in her veins to delight in the uncertain future. "Mind!" she cried, and put away from her the heartbreaking thought of leaving the beloved old house. "Mind! Goodness, when do we leave?"

CHAPTER TWO

During the week following Mr. Callandar's departure with the will, a frown and a great many more words of disapproval, Capri one day rode up to the front steps on her bicycle and discovered a man sitting there in the sun.

"Hello," she said warily, propping her bicycle against the steps. "What can I do for you?"

"You may unlock the door at once," he said gratefully. "I'm extremely numb from sitting here so long."

Capri looked at him in astonishment. He was well over 6 feet tall, which meant that legs and all he completely barred her entrance to the house. He had sandy hair, a rather stern-looking face and an almost invisible sandy mustache.

"I'm sorry," she said. "If you want to burgle the house there's nothing left. It's for sale."

"For goodness' sake," said the stranger, I'm not at all interested in becoming a burglar. In fact, it's my duty to apprehend them. I want a look at your house. I am what you might call a prospective buyer."

"Oh, dear," said Capri, and promptly apologized. "I thought—-"

"Entirely my fault," said the gentleman, standing up and brushing off his trousers. "I arrived with a dour-faced old chap—-"

"That would be Mr. Callandar," said Capri immediately.

"Yes. Well, he went off to the barn to find you. I assumed you came from there."

"I didn't. But I can show you the house. My mother bicycled in the opposite direction to the store."

The gentlemen's eyebrows shot upwards. "Your mother bicycles?"

"We can't afford a car," said Capri briefly. And she added under her breath, "Not unless you bought the house, mister."

She escorted him through the empty rooms, and he acted just like all the others who had come to see the house. He examined beams and walls and floors as though he were an architect; he squinted and gauged as if he were planning to build an exact duplicate. Capri sighed and waited and at last piloted him into the big study.

"Well!" exclaimed the towering stranger. "Who in the world is this?"

He was staring at the life-size painting of the Abbots that now leaned haphazardly against the door.

"Why, that's Uncle Shoe and mother," explained Capri. She added with a touch of pride, "Perhaps you've heard of them -—Schumann and Francia Abbott?"

"Uh, no. That is, what did they do? Should I know them?"

Capri stole a furtive glance at her companion and decided it was unlikely that he had seen much vaudeville. She said regretfully, "No, I suppose not. They were in vaudeville years ago. "Uncle Shoe died just last week."

"And the gracious lady?"

Capri flushed. Her mother did look the gracious lady in the portrait. But, in real life, Francia was always too busy raising the leghorns and marketing the eggs; she was usually tired and a little cross, and very much like a vagabond in faded slacks and a sweater.

"That's mother."

"Aha," said the gentleman. "The cyclist. You live here too, then?"

"Oh yes," explained Capri, beginning to like him. "I've lived here all my life. Of course, before I was born Francia lived everywhere in the world. She and Uncle Shoe even gave a command performance for the king and queen of England."

"My, my," said her friend. "And did your father perform for royalty, too?"

"No. He worked in a bank." She did not tell him how distressing this seemed to her. It pleased Francia, but Capri thought it strange. "I never knew my father," she explained. "He was killed in a train accident. That's when uncle shoe took us in."

"A very queer place to hide lovely Miss Francia Abbott," mused the stranger. "Very queer."

Capri gave him a curious look and led him to the cellar.

"These canned pickles look delightful," he said.

"The beams are over a hundred years old," Capri pointed out.

But the stranger was more interested in the pickles. "Whose are these?" he asked. "Oh, my, and blueberries and mincemeat, too. Delicious."

"Well, they're mine and Frans," responded to Capri. "We put them up together."

"An odd relationship," said the man. "Did you actually run this old farm without help?"

She nodded. "Of course. After the money went we had to. Uncle Shoe owned it, we all repaired it and ran it." Her eyes kindled, remembering. "Fran and Uncle Shoe tried awfully hard, really they did. Uncle Shoe was the worst of us, though. He didn't know a thing about farms, but he thought it was very romantic to own one."

"It doesn't sound too successful, two theatricals running a farm."

Capri said honestly, "It wasn't. I suppose you ought to know that this would be a bad buy. The land's no good."

She was not at all conscience-stricken at telling him this. There was no reason to believe he would buy the farm. There had been so many prospective buyers the first few days that Fran had begun calling them PB's. But it was surprising how few of them were interested in a tumbledown farm, even if its fruit orchards bloomed like pink and white confetti in the spring and the lilacs along the drive were like fountains tossing lavender spray as tall as the house. It seemed that PB's whether short, lean or fat, demanded fruit to be born on those trees and more than lilacs for remembrance.

But the gentleman smiled at her. "I haven't as yet seen or heard a thing to discourage me."

Capri grinned back. "Don't say I didn't try."

They walked upstairs and discovered Mr. Callandar leaning against a trunk in the otherwise empty hall.

"Well, there you are!" he cried stiffly. "Really, sir, you slipped away. That is—-"

"Don't apologize," said the stranger. "I did slip away. Tried to. Snatched at the chance. I wanted to see the place for myself."

Mr. Callandar looked properly shocked. "Dear, dear," he murmured, "that's too bad. I wanted to point out the beams. Over a hundred years old you know. And the springhouse has quite a history."

"That's what I was afraid of," replied the stranger, smiling. And bringing out two white cards, he introduced himself as Joshua Gayfeather.

"Mr. Gayfeather from Canada City, eh," said Mr. Callandar suspiciously. "Yes. Well—-"

"Well, I'm interested," said Mr. Gayfeather, and Capri was quite as surprised as Mr. Callandar at this. "With a few accompanying terms, that is."

Mr. Callandar shook his head. "I warned you."

"They have nothing to do with you," replied Mr. Gayfeather rather coldly. "They are entirely up to Miss -—Miss—-"

"Capri Maccomb."

"Capri? An odd name."

"After the island. Fran visited there once. When she was wealthy."

Mr. Gayfeather's eyes twinkled. "I see," he said. "Well, I would like to purchase your farm providing—-"

"Yes?" whispered Capri, holding her breath.

"Providing the mincemeat, the blueberries, the pickles and one full-length portrait remain intact in the house."

Mr. Callandar moved uncomfortably. He wanted to jump at the offer, but it was apparent that he did not wish to seem too eager. "Well, Capri?" he asked formally.

"Why, I'm sure it's all right," Capri said, puzzled. "That is, where we are going, we couldn't possibly take them with us." She did not tell him where they were going; that was the one question he had not asked. She hoped Mr. Callandar would not tell him, either; it made them sound too desperate.

"Then the place is mine." Mr. Gayfeather drew a deep breath; his eyes were sparkling. "Oh, those lilacs!" he murmured. "Beautiful. When may we move in?"

Mr. Callandar looked crafty. "I dare say your wife—-"

"Housekeeper," amended Mr. Gayfeather. "I'm not married."

"Well, your housekeeper will want to clean the place up a bit, but—-"

"We'd be glad to move out tomorrow," Capri broke in eagerly. "Frans been dying to start. Everything's packed. We've been living out of suitcases."

"And where are you going?" asked Mr. Gayfeather at last.

"Shall we go to my office now?" suggested Mr. Callandar hastily, and Capri grinned at his shocked demeanor. She followed him down the drive to Mr. Callandar's automobile. With one foot on the running board Mr. Gayfeather turned.

"Drop in some time," he said. "You must. When the place is mine."

Capri winced. He couldn't possibly understand how she felt about leaving. It was quite possible that Fran did not understand, either. After all, Fran had lived many, many places but for Capri there had only been one home.

"Of course," Capri said politely. "We'd love to."

She watched the car disappear down the lonely country road. Then she turned and scuffed her way moodily back to the house. Fran's bicycle leaned against the beech tree; Fran herself was staggering toward the porch with an enormous bundle of groceries.

"We won't need them," Capri said soberly. "The house has just been sold."

"No!" Fran sat down on the steps, and a can of beans rolled across the grass. "Oh, drat it," she said, and suddenly Capri knew that it mattered to her, too.

Fran glanced up and blinked away her tears. "Well, let's have a celebration," she said, and straightened her shoulders. "I bought some canned lobster. Can you imagine such extravagance? I never dreamed—-" She was going to cry again.

"We'll have a party in Uncle Shoe's study," said Capri. "With candles, and all the windows opened."

"And the lilacs streaming in!"

They hastened to the kitchen to steam the lobster and select a sauce. Then Fran made Capri sit on a stool and tell her all about Mr. Gayfeather's call. Did he notice the lilacs and the missing backstep? And Capri carefully included the story of the pickles and the mincemeat. They talked and made plans and occasionally stirred the lobster, now bubbling on the stove, and all the time they knew they were only trying to comfort one another. They were startled when the doorbell rang. It was five o'clock.

"Perhaps Mr. Callandar," suggested Fran.

"Does he want blood?" said Capri crossly. "Please don't invite him to dinner."

"Goodness, no!" cried Francia.

But it was not Mr. Callandar. It was a delivery boy from the local florist shop. He carried in his arms an enormous bouquet of cut flowers.

"For Capri Maccomb," he announced.

"Me?" Capri accepted wonderingly, and Francia unwrapped them.

"Why, they're from Mr. Gayfeather," she said. "Because of the pickles."

This set Mr. Gayfeather apart so definitely from all the other PB's that Capri realized with dismay that she would have to remember him for some time to come. She was sorry. She wanted to forget the new landlord who was about to trespass on what had been theirs.

15

"If we can't take the pickles and mincemeat with us, what does he expect me to do with flowers?"

"But isn't it nice of him," breathed Francia.

"Nice!" wailed Capri. "N—-nice?" And she promptly burst into tears. Their party was ruined.

CHAPTER THREE

They had checked out of a dingy hotel room ugly with olive-drab curtains and a faded pink chair. Francia was certain there were mice in the walls but the sheets were clean and the price for one night was two dollars. If Capri had been tempted to feel wealthy after the sale of the house to Mr. Gayfeather, she was now wholly subdued, for the ultimate sum of money which had reached them, once the mortgage and their creditors had been paid off, was very little, indeed, for two people starting a new life.

"Nor does it truly belong to us," Francia had explained. "It belongs to our carnival, and each penny must go into the carnival in such a manner that it magically comes out a dollar. In polite circles that's called economics, but for you and me it's sheer desperation."

It was the beginning of a new, tighter economy that might have depressed them both exceedingly, but the long dark ride from the city and the clean cold night air from the mountains were like a tranquil finger on Capri's pulse. She was beginning to enjoy herself.

Already they could see and dimly hear the carnival down the road. The country night was black, blacker than a cave, but up ahead the spotlights from the carnival moved heavenward like yellow paper streamers stretched from the earth to the sky.

"Not so much doin' tonight," volunteered their bus driver. "Last night the police raided it, but you'll be safe. Lightning never strikes twice, they say."

"How nice," Fran said grimly. "How lovely."

"Oh, the police always raid this kind of carnival; they got to, once or twice. But it scares away the tourist; they come for the thrills, but not that kind of thrill." The driver threw a speculative glance at Fran and Capri, his eyes price tagging their smart new suits. Capri caught his eye and grinned at him, and he had the grace to flush.

"Just the same it's too bad you don't have a man with you," he went on. "Lady just the other night had her purse snatched in there and couldn't pay her bus fare."

"Do we get off here?" asked Francia sternly.

"That's right, lady." They drew up beneath an enormous elm by the side of the road. "Bus stops on the other side going back."

Capri thanked him and followed her mother down the steps. Then the bus pulled away, leaving them with a first glimpse of their new home.

CARNIVAL GYPSY

The carnival burst upon them with all the suddenness of a circus parade rounding a corner. It assaulted their eardrums and hurt their eyes; it quickened their pulse and overwhelmed their senses. There were the sounds of a dozen barkers hawking their wares over tinny microphones, there was ceaseless grinding of the whip and the Ferris wheel, the gay thump of calliope music and an occasional scream from the faint hearted.

The smells were pungent --—hot buttered popcorn, sawdust, oil, dirt and, from somewhere to the east, the nostalgic scent of honeysuckle.

Capri glanced around with a starry-eyed appreciation. She saw a makeshift wall of crimson wagons and tall canvas screens lavishly decorated with faded pictures. Around each light bulb strung across the entrance swam a gauzy wreath of insects.

"Two," said Fran.

The man in the striped wooden box slid two orange tickets towards them and quickly gestured them past. They moved on, caught up in the press of the crowd.

Within the gates it was a bedlam of music and noise. Capri grasped her mother's hand firmly; if it was indeed an off night, as the bus driver had suggested, the sounds of the carnival were determined to dispel any such hint of defeat --—the voices of the people who walked around and around the sawdust path were pitched to a shout.

"It's a lovely carnival," Capri said ecstatically. "Just lovely, Fran."

Francia gave her an amused glance. "Then you've never seen a big-time show, darling. Just listen to that calliope music, it skips a note every three bars. And I wonder if anyone has thought of using fresh paint here in over ten years!"

"But it's ours. It is, isn't it, Fran?"

"The rides are, but I wouldn't care to sample them. The rest are concessions."

"But what do they sell at the concessions?" asked Capri. "Look at all the booths packed side by side like sardines."

"Chances. Those are the wheels of fortune," explained Francia mercilessly. "The empty ones are probably closed because of last night's raid. Their proprietors are no doubt still in jail."

"Oh," Capri said weakly, and turned to the center where the sports seemed of a more wholesome air. There was a Whip, a Loop O-Plane, a small merry-go-round filled with shouting children, and an enormous airplane swing that sent its travelers flying far up into the night.

"That looks like fun," she volunteered.

They passed the tall man in a bowler hat who was persuading the public they must see Ten Tall Terrific Dancing Girls flown straight from the Magic Isle of Oahu to perform a newly discovered native dance.

Francia sighed. They went on to a Bingo tent, and at last came to rest at one of the small dim cubicles that dotted the grounds.

The booth was almost deserted now. A young man was wearily, methodically throwing balls at an effigy of Adolf Hitler and tipping it over every time.

"See how easy it is, kid?" he asked of a small boy who watched at his side. "Just come to Jack Last's booth to win the prizes."

"Gee, yeah," said the boy, squirming with excitement. The back of his leather jacket showed that he was a member of a

Superman Club and his name, clumsily stenciled in white, was Billy. "Gee, whaddya think, Betsy?" he asked.

His sister, whom he held tenderly by the hand, was a more cautious nature. Now she nodded vigorously, "Yes," she whispered. "Yes."

"Well, what shall we try for? What prize?"

Together they searched the shelves that bulged with possibilities. But the eyes of Betsy had come upon a vision of a doll dressed in starched pink organdy and real blonde hair. She caught her breath and pointed a finger at.

"Yeah, that's pretty," said Billy. "But you maybe wouldn't prefer a radio?"

Betsy's gaze flickered politely over the radio but returned to the doll.

"Okay, the doll," Billy told Jack Last. She's only got a little old thing we patched up with chewing gum. Can we try for the doll?"

"Sure, sure, easy," said the young man. "But it'll cost you ten cents for three balls."

Billy's fingers retreated to his pocket. He drew out a thin solitary dime. "There," he said, much too casually, his eyes bidding it farewell.

"The young man named Jack Last took the dime, flipped it expertly in the air, placed it in his pocket, and offered Billy his three balls. "Go ahead, kid," he said, turned away indifferently.

Billy squinted at Adolf Hitler, aimed the ball and threw. The ball spun wide and hit the canvas, knocking down only clouds of dust.

Capri said, drawing closer, "Throw it harder." And to Betsy, smiling, she said, "He's got a fast pitch."

"Oh, he's wonderful," explained his sister. "At home he can hit anything."

But Billy was clearly not at home now. His second ball plummeted crazily to the ground. Billy drew back and wiped the perspiration from his brow. "Gee," he said, "I don't know what's the matter with me."

"It's our only dime," cried Betsy bewilderingly, her lower lip trembling.

From behind them Francia said coldly, try another ball, Billy. Try one of the balls the young man was using. And she walked contemptuously behind the counter to pluck one off the shelf.

"Hey, get out of there," shouted Jack Last. "Who do you think you are?"

He received a look of such scorn that he closed his mouth with a snap.

"Go ahead now," counseled Fran. Billy did, and it hit Adolf Hitler squarely in the eye.

"All right, give him the doll," said Fran.

"He gets no doll," snarled Jack Last. "He only hit him once. You got to hit it three times to get a prize."

"Those first two balls were duds," Fran said, and Capri had never seen her so furious. "He couldn't have hit a barn door with them. Give him that doll and get rid of those fakes. Do you hear me?"

"Oh, yeah?" The young man faced her menacingly, his hands on his hips. "And who says so? You get out of here or I'll call the boss."

Francia laughed. "Go right ahead."

Placing two fingers in his mouth Jack Last drew a piercing whistle. Fran leaned over and reached for the doll. "There, Billy," she said gently, "there's your prize. Run along and be more careful after this."

"I can have it fair and square?" faltered Billy.

"Fair and square," repeated Fran.

"Gee, Billy," sighed Betsy accepting this armful of ruffles and curls. "Gee!"

Jack Last said ominously, "The kid leaves the carny with that doll and he's a thief."

Francia tapped her foot impatiently. "I'm still waiting for your boss," she reminded him.

Behind her someone coughed, both Capri and Francia turned. A stout man with a pink, heavily chinned face and rubbery lips stood at their elbow. "I'm sorry," he said in a soft suave voice, "but the doll will cost you ten dollars if you insist upon the child winning it."

"And who are you?" asked Fran.

"If you plan to make trouble," said the stranger, "I shall have to ask you to leave." He glanced speculatively at the crowd that was beginning to gather.

"I asked who you were," repeated Fran.

The stout man bowed, his eyes full of amusement. "I am Nicholas H. Sabo, acting manager of the Toby Brothers Traveling Show."

Fran said crisply, "Your young man here runs a crooked business. He throws the good balls himself as a come-on. The customer gets nothing but duds."

Mr. Sabo's eyes narrowed. "You're making an accusation which I trust you can prove?" His glance flicked casually beyond Capri to Jack Last. He gave an imperceptible signal.

Fran said, "I saw that. You needn't try to hide those dud balls."

Mr. Sabo laughed unpleasantly. "All right, lady," he said, "you've made enough mischief. Take the doll and those kids and get out of here. Head straight for the gate and don't come back. I run an honest carnival. I don't have to put up with this."

"You do not run an honest carnival," said Francia, "and you will have to put up with this. You see, I'm the new owner."

There was a confused silence. Mr. Sabo said, "You're what?"

"I am Francia Abbott Maccomb, owner of the Toby Brothers Traveling Show," she announced, parodying his own words. "Surely you received word of my brother's death?"

Jack Last said uneasily, "She's kidding, ain't she, boss? Say the word and I'll call a copper."

Mr. Sabo brushed his words aside impatiently. "Something must have gone wrong," he said. "You did not receive my offer to buy the carnival?"

Fran nodded. "Yes, we received it."

Mr. Sabo stared at her angrily for a long moment. "I see," he said at last. A muscle flexed in his jaw. "The children can have the doll, of course, then," he said. "You must forgive me. Yes." His flat lips parted in a grotesque smile. "If you will come to the office, Mrs. Maccomb?"

"Good-bye, Billy," said Capri. "Goodbye, Betsy."

Betsy gave the doll an extra little hug; its hair tickled her nose and she sneezed.

"Thanks a million," said Billy. "C'mon now, we got to go."

Capri turned to Mr. Sabo. With a savage, ironic bow, he guided them stiffly away from the scene.

CHAPTER FOUR

Mr. Sabo led Francia and Capri through the crowds and away from the immediate circle of light. Then he disappeared among the canvas backdrops and, following him, they found themselves in the darkness at the foot of a long, gently swelling hill. Somewhere nearby a dynamo throbbed. The low hum of the carnival was muted, punctuated sharply by screams from the Ferris wheel that rose almost over their heads. But the immediate noises were replaced by the kinder sounds of crickets in the grass and the lapping of waves against a far-off beach.

"This way," said Mr. Sabo stiffly. "The trailers—-" He finished his sentence by gesture. They saw that half a dozen trailers lay before them in the darkness. To their right the small mountain lake narrowed itself into an inlet that curved like a crooked finger to the very foot of the carnival field.

"This is mine. That is, it belongs to the manager," said Mr. Sabo, an unlocked the door of a long, stream-lined silver trailer.

"Capri—-" said Fran.

"I'll sit outside on the steps," Capri said.

She sat down, first testing the step with the finger to find it clean. When her mother had gone inside, Capri leaned forward and rested her head in her hands. The night air was soft to her face; the quick little breeze from the lake brought with it the damp smell of fog. Farther up the hill someone emptied a pail of water in the grass, slamming the door shut behind them; Capri jumped as Mr. Sabo opened a window over her head. Voices at once drifted out to her.

"You mean that you and your daughter are going to *stay*?" She heard Mr. Sabo say. He sounded flabbergasted, as though this had not occurred to him.

"Yes," came Fran's voice coldly, "it's all we have left. Naturally, I shall manage it now."

There was the sound of Mr. Sabo lowering his vast bulk into a chair. "You're joking," he said. "A carnival is no place for a woman and a girl."

Fran's voice came from a distance, as though she had turned away. "I shall make it a place for myself in Capri, Mr. Sabo.

"But what do you know about running a carny? Why, you'll be bankrupt in a month. The concessionaires will cheat you as soon as they hear about this; you'll get scarcely a cent from them. I beg of you, Mrs. Maccomb, allow me to buy the show from you."

"If by concessionaires," said Francia calmly, "you mean those dishonest men down there, I shall be rid of them before they learn about our arrival."

"Then you'll be bankrupt in a week," said Mr.' Sabo.

Francia said silkily, "It is really none of your business, Mr. Sabo. Capri and I shall move into this trailer tomorrow."

"You're dismissing me?"

"Yes."

Mr. Sabo's voice was more suave. "Then I must remind you that both merry go rounds leave, too. They belong to me. Mr. Abbott only leased them."

Something dropped inside the trailer. Fran said in a small, odd voice, "I didn't know that."

"You do now." It was a thinly veiled challenge.

"Would you stay on to run the merry go rounds?" asked Francia.

"I should certainly dislike leaving," said Mr. Sabo.

Fran hesitated; then she said in her usual voice, "That means that you will remain, and I'm not unhappy about that, Mr. Sabo. There will be many times I shall need your advice and help. Yes, I'm glad you will still be with us". But her voice sounded to Capri a trifle dubious, as though she was weighing Mr. Sabo's established authority against that of her own, a stranger.

"Thank you," said Mr. Sabo courteously.

"Now, if you would be so kind, if you could tell me something about the carnival—-"

"Of course," said Mr. Sabo briskly. "You already know that it's a gilly show -—that is, its truck transported. We remain here for the week; our next stop is Oak Hills and then Tuttling Mills. We're not allowed in the larger towns.

Outside, leaning against the top step of the trailer, Capri sighed, obscurely troubled by the change she had sensed in Francia ever since they stepped inside the gates ——a change substantiated by the manner in which Francia was dealing with Mr. Sabo. At the farm they had always been close, she and Francia and Uncle Shoe, but between Capri and her mother there had flourished the delightful companionship of two sisters. Tonight, this quality was missing. It was as though, from the moment they entered the carnival, Francia had withdrawn from Capri, sloughing off the old relationship, tightening her authority, becoming distant and much less fun. What had happened, Capri realized with a shock, was that suddenly, without warning, Francia had ceased being a sister and had become her mother again.

Capri sat quietly, absorbing this strange discovery. She was not dismayed so much as she was saddened——it meant that for Francia there promised to be no adventure in managing a carnival; to her it had to be a cold, hard business proposition. And Capri wondered why, for this was so unlike her. Francia was accustomed to extracting the last ounce of fun from even the most difficult of situations.

Of course, she's tired. Perhaps that s it, Capri thought, watching the Ferris wheel pause for a moment like a round golden moon over the rooftops of the carnival. Uncle Shoe's death was a great shock, and then seeing the farm go ——Uncle Shoe spoiled us both so dreadfully, and now she has to pull herself together and find new security for us.

But that was not solely the trouble. She doesn't like the carnival, Capri realized. It must be different than what she expected, or else she doesn't like it because of me. I wish I knew. But something's made her change.

Capri stood up. Her foot had gone to sleep, leaving an unpleasant tickle in her leg. With little hops and jumps she walked down the hill. The grass had grown damp to the touch as the mist from the lake moved in, but there was a tiny path shining faintly in the light as she pursued it stubbornly, not realizing that she was being followed.

Suddenly, with the impact of an avalanche, Capri was thrown to the ground. She tasted earth and weeds, and lay too stunned to move. A rough mackinaw jacket brushed her face; A figure bent over her.

"Listen, you townie, didn't I tell you to quit sneaking into the carnival? Didn't I? And this is just a sample of what you'll get if I catch you doing it again. Do you hear me?"

Capri managed to nod her head. The hard grip on her back relaxed. She was suddenly released.

"Okay, then. Get up and get out of here."

Capri sat up and drew a deep breath. She was all right; one knee was bruised and she was painfully dizzy, but her bones were unbroken. She became gradually aware of a pair of wide masculine shoulders looming black against the sky. She shook her head to clear it and saw that her assailant was sitting back on his heels staring at her aghast.

"Jumping catfish, a girl!"

"And who did you think I was?" gasped Capri.

The shadow moved and, in the patch of light that striped his shoulders, Capri saw for the first time that the boy was young, not so much older than she. In the darkness his face was only a series of jutting planes, like steps cut from a rock, but there was an innocence about his jaw that gave away his youthfulness.

"I'm sorry," he said. "I thought you were the fellow who's been sneaking in every night. Fellow from the lake. He has plenty of money to spend, but he's got to steal his way in every time." He rubbed his jaw softly. "I should have known," he added. "You went over too easy."

"It didn't feel that way to me," she said ruefully. "You almost broke my neck."

He held out his hand and swung her to her feet effortlessly. They stared at one another curiously for a moment. The lines of his face were clear-cut and strong; his eyes glittered like blonde marbles under straight brows. In the shabby plaid mackinaw and faded dungarees, he was like a young Atlas in masquerade.

"I must say you're loyal to the carnival," she said.

He shrugged. "I work here. I'm a roustabout. One place is as good as another."

"A roustabout?" she faltered.

"Sure. We pack away the show every Sunday. Take it down. Put it up."

"But why a carnival if one place is as good as another?"

Again he shrugged. "Maybe I just happen to like carnivals."

Capri turned her face toward the umbrella of light over their heads. The continuous noise was like the drone of a hundred radios, each tuned to a different station and slightly off key, but to her ears it rang true, it was music. "I don't blame you," she said wonderingly, her face aglow. "I don't blame you at all."

The boy stared at her as though trying to memorize her features. Then, without another word, he suddenly turned on his heel and disappeared into the shrubbery. She could hear his footsteps all the way back to the carnival; then the sounds quieted and vanished and once again the crickets took over the night. A grackle shrilled at her from a tree. Something formless and eerie slithered across the path into the deeper grass.

With a little cry, Capri ran back up the slope of the hill toward the trailer. She was suddenly aware of the darkness, of the cold brooding sky overhead, and the feeling of a storm in the air. The sounds of the carnival grew too loud to her ears. She ran as though pursued by them.

CHAPTER FIVE

Mr. Sabo closed the door of his trailer softly behind him and, with the grace that is often worn by stout men, he walked quickly down the hill in the direction of the carnival. It was close to midnight. Mrs. Maccomb and her daughter had returned to their lodgings in the city, and Mr. Sabo had work to do. He knew exactly where he was going and whom he must see; his mission, in fact, had been clear to him from the moment that he had been told he was no longer in charge of the Toby Brothers Traveling Show. Only Mr. Sabo knew what an effort it had cost him to keep his wits upon receiving such a shock, but now his wrath was unfettered. Over his head the spotlights swung 'round and 'round in a vivid arc; the clouds they pointed up were rain clouds, but the carnival had made a great deal of money tonight, despite what he had told Francia.

A little rain now would do business no harm, providing it stopped before dawn.

He made his way through the crowd, looking neither to the right nor to the left. Only when he came to Jack Last's booth did he pause. Jack had another boy in with him tonight, a tall, broad-shouldered boy, with an easy grace and a shuttered face, one of the newer roustabouts, Mr. Sabo remembered, looking him over sharply. The boy's honesty was as yet unprobed, but the very fact that he was a roustabout was sufficient. The clincher was that he was Jack's friend.

Mr. Sabo moved forward and gave Jack a nod. "Don't go," he said to the other young man. "Any friend of Jack's is a friend of mine.

"That's right," said Jack, "he's okay. Matt, you know Mr. Sabo?"

Matt came forward and leaned on the counter. "Oh, yes," he said.

"Good. I've got a little work for you boys."

"What kind of work?" asked Matt with interest.

Jack grinned wickedly. "Thought you got your walking papers tonight, boss. Didn't you hear the little lady? 'I'm Francia Abbott Maccomb!'" he mimicked and burst into a guffaw.

Both Matt and Mr. Sabo looked startled, but it was Matt who spoke. "What do you mean?" he asked, "Mr. Sabo owns the show, doesn't he?"

Mr. Sabo bit his lip in irritation. "Not exactly, Matt."

"Naw," broke in Jack, "he just runs it. We got a new owner now, and this'll give you a laugh. It's a *woman*. Some lady and her daughter. The kids not bad."

"She wouldn't be blonde, would she," said Matt slowly, "maybe a couple of years younger than you and me, and she had a pink suit on tonight?"

Jack's mouth dropped open. "That's her. You meet her already?"

Matt nodded. "In a way I met her, yes."

"Well, they're the two that gave Mr. Sabo such a time of it. Eh, boss?"

"I wasn't conscious of it," Mr. Sabo said smoothly. "Has anyone ever gotten the best of Nicholas Sabo?"

Jack sobered immediately. "You're right there, boss. What can we do for you?"

"I'd like you to go back to your old job for a while, Jack."

"Aw gee, boss, you know I'd rather stay here. This is plenty soft, and the money's good. The other just ain't my line of work, tangling with the copper so much."

Mr. Sabo's eyes twinkled pleasantly. "But you're uncommonly good at it. Would it help if I said you could keep every cent you get?"

Jack whistled. "I don't get it. Where's the profit for you?"

Mr. Sabo leaned forward; a muscle twitched in his cheek. He said in a harsh, furious voice, "I want trouble made. I want plenty of trouble made. You understand? We'll keep this between us three. Your friend Matt will take this booth while you're making the rounds."

A blinding light dawned on Jack's face. "I get it," he cried. "The little lady doesn't approve of pickpockets!"

Mr. Sabo nodded. "That alright with you, Matt?"

Matt frowned. "I'll certainly take the booth for Jack, but I don't know as I—"

Jack Last dug his elbow into his friend's arm. "Skip it, Matt. Skip it, you hear me?"

Mr. Sabo gave Jack a sharp glance. "I thought you said your friend was squared."

"Sure, sure, boss," Jack said uneasily. "He'll go along with us. He doesn't owe anybody any money at this carny."

"Very well. I'll hold you responsible for him." Mr. Sabo walked away. But he did not return immediately to his trailer. He stopped here and there at several different booths and exchanged words with quite a few of his more trusted friends.

CHAPTER SIX

It was almost noon. The lake was chased with angry whitecaps driven furiously by a north wind. But the sun was warm. Capri emptied her bucket of soapsuds in a thicket and watched them evaporate. That was the last of that, she thought grimly. It was surprising how seldom Mr. Sabo had scrubbed his floors, but the trailer was theirs now and Mr. Sabo had retreated to a smaller abode to work his will upon four fresh walls.

"So you're the new young 'un," said a kindly voice behind her. Capri turned. An extravagant shape of a man stood watching her. He looked like a gypsy, his teeth flashing white against his gaunt brown face. As she smiled, he came forward sticking out a great brown hand.

"Doc Boone's the name," he said. "I can fix any machine in the world. That's my job. Glad to meet you."

Capri grinned. "My name's Capri Maccomb," she said, and placed her own hand in the larger one, wincing at his firm clasp.

He looked her over with delight. "See you got your dungarees as weathered as mine," he said. "Now that's a queer name you own. You a theatrical?"

"No, but my mother used to be."

He scratched one ear thoughtfully. "Nick Sabo didn't tell me that. But Nick Sabo doesn't know everything, now does he. Heard you were a couple of greenhorns, so I thought I'd come round and help you out."

Capri laughed. "I guess we are greenhorns. We hoped nobody would find out. But it's certainly nice of you to come around."

"Look," he said, "there's not a window in these trailers that's not busy. Carny folk are mighty clannish and suspicious of townies. Word got around, you know, and it was Nick Sabo's word, too. He's got no use for anyone but Nick Sabo. Why don't you come over and meet my mother? She's dyin' to see you."

Capri was grateful. The circle of trailers on the hill had seemed as aloof and unfriendly as a graveyard. "I'd love to, Mr. Boone," she said, falling into step with him.

"Now don't go callin' me *that*," he said reproachfully. "No need for formality. Me and Ma are two of the regulars, we're with you 'til the carny closes. Doc's the name."

They crossed deep grass to approach his trailer. Immediately Capri saw that it was neater than the others; its paint was fresh and there was a bright and shiny galvanized pale by the door with the brick to hold down its lid.

"You come right in," Doc said. "Ma, put a kettle of hot water on, I brought you company just like you asked. My mother's associable one all right," he chuckled.

Capri took one step inside and almost laughed aloud. It was incredible what had happened to the interior of the trailer -—a deft hand had changed it into a little old lady's parlor. There were heavily starched lace curtains at the windows, a pot of geraniums and a dozen china dogs on the whatnot, and in the center of the room in a rocking chair sat a lady with blue-black hair parted exquisitely in the center of her head, and beady black eyes as young and mischievous as it girl's. She was wrapped from head to foot in a black cape and wore long, glittering silver earrings.

At the sight of Capri, Doc's mother let out a shout. "Tarnation, Boone," she cried in a hoarse voice, "she's a pretty one, all right. Pour the water, Boone, and we'll have some tea. Sit down, deary. Well!"

Capri smiled and lowered herself into a chair.

"Now tell me right away when your birthday is, dearie."

Capri was taken aback. Why, it's in June.

Doc's mother nodded her head vigorously. "That's good, that's good. I'll look it up tonight. But I *know* yesterday was a most auspicious day for a change under the sign of Cancer. You'll do, you'll do, child. Where is your mother?"

"Her name's Capri," volunteered Doc from the tiny kitchen.

"She went to town," said Capri. "We left two suitcases behind."

Mrs. Boone nodded and, seeing that the tea was ready, she reached out and with one great swoop that belied her fragility

39

brought to her side a small table. "Put 'em here, dearie," she told Doc. "Lemon, sugar, cream?"

Capri said weakly, "Lemon, please." She loathed tea, but she accepted the cup and spooned it politely.

"Well, now," said Mrs. Boone, settling herself comfortably. Suddenly she tilted her head to one side and stared brightly. "And what do you think of the Carny, dear?"

"I don't really know yet," replied Capri, honestly enough.

Ma Boone leaned back again. "Just a small-time gilly show, that's what it is. But mark my words, dearie, it's high time Nick Sabo went back to his merry-go-rounds and let somebody else manage for a change." She chuckled. "Does my heart good to see him kicked out of that trailer. He went to great pains choosin' it, he did; picked out the biggest, most expensive one he could find, when all the time it wasn't his money that paid for it, 'twas your uncle's. Wasn't that right, Boone?"

"Whatever you say, Ma," said Doc, his eyes twinkling.

"Boone and I have worked them all," went on Mrs. Boone serenely. "But I must say this carny's the limit. Your Ma'll give it class, I hope." She leaned forward in her voice became confidential. "There's hanky-panky's and strong games -—but this carny's got more strong games than you can shake a cop at. I warned Nick he couldn't go on patching the law forever."

Capri laughed. "What in the world does that mean?"

Doc grinned. "Ma picks up all the jargon. Hanky-panky's are the ten-cent-or-less games. Like where you pitch pennies on a floor to get 'em in a numbered circle. Didn't you see that? The strong games start at twenty-five cents and the sky's the limit. As for a patch, he's the carny's legal man. Everybody pays him to make sure he keeps 'em out of trouble. Nick does that kind of work, too."

"What else does he do?" asked Capri timidly.

"Why, he sees to the lights, arranges transportation, and rents the lots ahead of time. He pays a man to stay on the road putting up posters -—or did. Your Ma'll take over that now."

At the look of doubt and perplexity on Capri's face, they both burst out laughing. "Never mind," said Ma Boone, "the carny will run itself for awhile, and she'll be getting rid of the grifters. Your Ma looked mighty pretty; saw you both at Jack Last's booth last night."

"You work at the carnival, too?" Capri asked surprised.

Ma tells fortunes," said Doc drily, leaning against a buffet which sported a wreath of dried flowers captured under a bell-shaped glass. The corners of his mouth turned down wryly. "She could also be a wrestler if she wanted. And at her age, too. Don't let her fool you."

Ma Boone laughed, showing two neat rows of china teeth. "Get along with you, Boone," she said. "Finished your tea, dearie? I always say a spot of tea is warming. Give me your cup, that's it." She grasped the cup that Capri had gallantly emptied, and studied it, making quite a show with scowls and gestures.

"Well!" she exclaimed and gave Capri a knowing look. "I must say the stars were wrong."

"What do you mean, Mrs. Boone?" smiled Capri.

She placed the cup on the table and clicked her teeth. "You've some bad luck ahead, that's what my tea leaves say. My tea leaves never lie."

"Not much they don't," said Doc. "Why can't you tell her something nice?" He turned to Capri and shook his head.

"Ma's a nut on tea leaves. Don't pay her a bit of attention, it'll go to her head.'

Mrs. Boone's eyes rested on Capri with interest. "She's a nice girl, Boone. I like her." To Capri she said jauntily, "Come and see me tonight. It's the tent next to Jack's. Madam Zela, that's me. Nothing gypsy about me -—it's strictly class. And now I've got to be getting dressed, dearie." She rose, her skirts rustling like water, and poked a finger into Capri's hand. It was like being dismissed by a queen. Capri had the instinctive urge to curtsy, but restrained herself in time and compromised with a smile.

"You'll be all right now," said Doc, walking with her down the path. "I don't want to sound proud, but when Ma takes a fancy to someone, they're in. She liked you. Pretty soon you'll know everybody. The nice ones, anyhow."

"What about the bad ones?" asked Capri."

Doc gave her an amused glance. "You don't know carnies, do you? I'll tell you, though, there's a lot of riffraff in this one. "That's what Ma means. There's good carny folk and bad carny folk, but Nick Sabo never cared which he was hiring just so long as he got his percentage from 'em -—if he could. Anybody tries to make a sucker out of you, well, you just tell 'em you're with it. That's the word -—with it. They'll know."

"Which are the bad ones? Asked Capri.

"Well," Doc shrugged, "there's all the fly-by-nights, here one week, gone the next. The ones out to make a quick dollar, with their cars parked right behind their tent in case somebody complains to the fuzz."

"Fuzz?"

"The policeman at the carnival. There's always one."

"Oh. Well, do you mean bad ones like Jack Last?" asked Capri, remembering his dud balls.

Doc looked uneasy. Oh, Jack's all right," he said. "Look here, Capri," he went on awkwardly, "a carny's got to have *some* angles, you know. Can't make a fortune out of popcorn. People ask to be swindled."

Capri decided to think about this later; she could see that it was a wrong beginning.

"Look," said Doc, "I got to go down and check the transformer. Care to come along?"

Capri said she would love to go.

In the daylight the carnival had an innocent look; it appeared smaller and wholly subdued. A clean path of sawdust had been strewn over the midway, and if the paint was peeling in thick flakes from the canvas walls the gaudy colors emerged more purely under the sunlight and seemed less squalid than shabby. The dynamos in their big, red wheeled carts were well-oiled and beginning to hum. Over at the center Capri saw that Nick Sabo was starting up his merry-go-round; its mirrors glittered in the light and, as the machine began turning, a crescendo of gay music box melody filled the air and was abruptly stilled. Mr. Sabo smiled cheerfully at her, and Capri nodded in return.

Here's Ma's booth," said Doc proudly, and Capri was not surprised to see that it was as spruce as Mrs. Boone herself, with neatly lettered signs and an inviting dark interior.

"And here's the dancing girls' tent," said Doc. "You see 'em last night?"

Capri nodded her head. She hesitated, afraid of sounding foolish. "They aren't really from Hawaii, are they?"

Doc shouted with laughter. "I'll say they aren't. Here's Molly, she's in the show. You can judge for yourself. Hi, Molly, meet the new junior boss of the carny."

Molly was lying in a deck chair on the sunny side of the platform. She glanced up and smiled, her red hair falling over one eye. "Never been to Hawaii in my life," she said promptly, "but I sure wish I had. You showin' her around, Doc?"

"That's me, official guide. Molly here used to sing on Broadway 'til she lost her voice," he told Capri. "One of the best, too."

"Oh, the blarney of you," said Molly, pleased.

"Did she really?" asked Capri as they walked on. "Sing on Broadway, I mean?"

"She used to be a chorus girl," said Doc. "Led the line in every show, singing and dancing, you know. She wasn't just anybody, either -—every show she was ever in hit the jack pot. After a while all the producers wanted her in their musicals, kind of as a good luck token." He kicked absently at a piece of rope in their path. "But it wasn't her voice she lost, it was her looks. She got sick." He sighed. "That's what you get in a carny like this, people goin' up and people goin' down. But mostly down. And out," he added with a twisted smile. "They make a fortune in the summer, lose it all in the winter."

"What about you?" Capri asked candidly.

"Oh, me," he grinned. "I don't count. I'm no carnival guy. I'm a mechanic. I'm here just cuz' Ma's here." His grin deepened. "Ma retired when the old man died. Bought a little house in Albany and sat there waitin' to die until one day she said she couldn't stand it a second longer. So here we are. Ma's happy, and I came along to kind of look out for her."

"That's nice," said Capri.

"Yep, works out fine." Shading his hand, Doc glanced ahead of them. Capri followed his gaze and saw a familiar figure winding up a length of rope in the center of the midway. She said, 'Who's that fellow over there near the merry-go-round?"

Doc looked at her sharply, "Just another roustabout. You don't know him?"

She nodded. "I talked to him last night."

Doc looked uneasy. "Well, he's a friend of Jack Last's. Matt Lincoln's his name, I think. Hey, Matt," he called.

At Doc's words the boy paused and came forward, rolling down the sleeves of his turtleneck sweater. He walked with an easy, graceful stride. His tousled brown hair was bleached yellow, his face was deeply tanned. "Yes? he said politely.

"The new owner's daughter wanted to meet you. Capri Maccomb her name is."

Matt stood obediently still; his face indifferent to them both. The feeling of enmity between him and Doc made the air crackle.

"All right," said Doc, "you can run along. You want to watch out for the roustabouts," Doc said as they strolled on. "It pays not to bother 'em. They're a bunch of no-good hoodlums."

Capri turned and saw that Matt Lincoln was looking back, too. It was quite probable that he had heard every word: she blushed for him.

"Well, there's your ma," said Doc.

Capri glanced or the entrance. Francia was walking through the gate, chic and comfortable in well-cut slacks. A small boy followed her, carrying their suitcases. Seeing her return Capri felt a tremor of happiness run through her. With a new friend beside her, with the evening show coming on, the carnival drowsily awakening once more, and Francia back from town, it felt like home. A strange home but a welcomed one.

CHAPTER SEVEN

"Now what must we do," said Francia, "is get rid of the dancing girls and, of course, the wheels of fortune."

Capri leaned against the open door and nibbled peacefully on a blade of grass. Behind her sat Francia in the tiny office fashioned from one end of their trailer. With a sheaf of papers before her on the desk she looked extremely efficient.

"Fran," said Capri dreamily, "do you know what a patch is?"

"Of course," said Francia impatiently. "Clothes are patched."

Capri grinned and sat down on the steps. "What do you plan to replace the wheels with?"

Francia frowned. "Plenty. Only they cost money. Listen to this, darling, there's a motorcycle show that's looking for a place to come to roost. Trick riders, you know, and lots of noise. A carnival needs noise. They're good; they're used to better places than this, of course."

Capri laughed. "Now what can you mean, better places than this?"

Francia made a face. "You ought to see by now why this carnival never made Mr. Sabo or Shoe any money."

"What do these motorcyclists do?"

"Well," said Fran vaguely, "they have a portable motordrome with round walls. They ride around on the walls —without hands, too."

"Would they come to a little carnival like this?"

"If we offered them more money they would. And what a crowd they'd bring in!" She rustled her papers wistfully. "There's also a fellow here who dives 100 feet into a tank of water 6 feet deep. Wish we could afford him as a free act."

"I don't," said Capri, shuttering. "He might kill himself."

Francia laid down the papers and leaned back, closing her eyes. She said slowly, "I'll wire the motorcycle act. Captain Southland the man calls himself. Oh, Capri—-" Her eyes flew open suddenly. "If we could just clean up the carnival and play the big towns, places like Canada City, then we'd make money. Then we'd be free."

Capri said slowly, "You don't like the carnival, do you, Fran."

Francia's fingers tightened around the pencil she was holding. "I'm sorry," she said simply. "It's so shoddy, I can't wait to change it. The roustabouts look disreputable."

This shocked Capri. "Oh, Fran, I'm sure you're wrong. They may dress queerly, but they're polite and nice." She hesitated. "At least one of them is," she added.

Francia said, "You're scarcely a judge, darling. You've lived a very sheltered life."

Capri had an idea. "Fran," she begged, "it's so hot in here. Why not leave the paperwork and walk down through the carnival?"

"I've a better thought," announced Fran. "Let's go for a swim in the lake."

"Oh, no, a walk," pleaded Capri. "We haven't seen half the shows."

Francia swung around to regard her intently. "You want me to meet these people who work for us, don't you. I'm sorry, Capri, but I'm not going to. In the first place, I shall be firing some of them within twenty-four hours and in the second place, I want as little to do with them as possible."

"Fran!"

Francia's eyes softened. "Don't be shocked, darling," she said. "I'm only doing it for your ultimate good. We're here to make a living. We *have* to make money. We're not here to enjoy ourselves or to start a new life -—this carnival is only a means to an end. I don't want you to grow attached to any of these people."

"But, Fran, why not?" asked Capri in surprise.

Francia hesitated. Then, in a firm, clear voice, she said, "Because they live a different kind of life, a life which would only be too easy for you to grow accustomed to. It's not an easy life, Capri, but from the outside it does look exciting. I have many things planned for you, darling -—for both of us -—but I will not have you live the way I did for so long."

Capri burst out laughing. "But, Fran, I'm only fifteen!"

Francia shook her head. "You forget that I began a career at that age. At eighteen I was the toast of New York, and at twenty-one I was touring the Continent. For you, Capri -—for you life has got to be different."

Capri frowned at her mother's seriousness. "But still I don't understand. You know I can't sing or dance, and I can't keep a tune at all. Why should you worry then about my acquiring a taste for this sort of life?"

"Never mind why," said Francia, tight-lipped. "Just try to remember how I feel." And turning away she made a pretense at shuffling through her papers. Capri waited, but Francia paid no attention to her; it soon became evident that she did not intend to. Presently, with a little sigh, Capri left the room.

Capri had brushed her hair until it shone like polished gold. She wore a fresh white blouse and a crimson skirt; her eyes were wide open to the excitement of the midway. Tonight she was celebrating the fact that the carnival belonged to them. Last night she had been only a visitor.

Ma Boone was sitting in front of her tent waiting for the throng to pause before her door. She was attired in a purple satin gown with long, green glass earrings touching her shoulders. Capri thought she looked very elegant; under the dim globe that burned over the tent's door, she seemed as wise and crafty as a medieval sorceress.

"Want your fortune told, dearie?" Ma called to Capri. "I'll do it for free, of course," she added. "Good for business."

Capri smiled. "Let me come back," she begged. "I want to have a look around. I haven't even seen the snakes yet."

Ma Boone nodded. "Half an hour and the water'll be hot for a quick cup of tea."

Capri shuttered delicately and kept on walking. At the snake tent she paid the price of admission to a young man who wore his hat precariously on the back of his head. For a few minutes she watched the snakes writhing about in their pit, and then went out.

"Do they ever get away?" she asked the young man.

He looked her over coldly, his hands on his hips. He pushed the hat still further back on his head. "What's it to you, kid?" he asked.

Capri felt suddenly mischievous. She bent close and whispered, "Where's the fuzz?"

"Huh?" said the boy.

"I'm with it." And leaving him with his mouth wide open, she again joined the stream of humanity that wandered past.

At one of the booths in the center of the midway she came to a pause. Quite a few other people had stopped here, too, for it was apparent that a shabby-looking woman was winning quite a bit of money and prizes from the sad-looking gentleman who ran the booth. "Step right up 'n' choose a number," the man was chanting in a monotonous voice. "Step right here an" choose a number."

The woman said breathlessly, "Thirteen."

The man next to Capri said uneasily, "She ought to stop playing while she's ahead."

The woman heard him; she turned and gave him a queer glance. "Thirteen," she repeated.

The wheel spun 'round and 'round. A tiny ripple of excitement passed over the crowd, drawing Capri into it. The wheel slowed, hovered for a moment on the number twelve, and at last came to rest on thirteen.

"Why look, she's won again," said the man next to Capri. The crowd fluttered and chirped. Capri saw that everyone watching felt happy for the shabby little woman -—they were taking in her skimpy cotton dress, the worn down shoes, and the attractive baby she carried in her arms.

"Thirteen," she said again. This time the crowd surged forward to place their quarters on the board, too. Capri drew her breath in sharply; the woman was going to play almost all the money she had won. A terrible doubt assailed her. What was it Doc had said? The strong games started with a quarter, and they were the dishonest games.

"Please," she heard herself saying, "please don't play it all!"

Behind her someone said, "You'd better be careful." She glanced up questioningly to find Matt Lincoln standing at her elbow, "Look, kid," he said, "come over here a minute."

She followed obediently. There was a reluctant smile of amusement in Matt's eyes as he turned to face her. "Look," he said, "the man who runs that booth is named Vincie Nebbs." He waited and she nodded. Then he added significantly, "The woman you saw playing -—well, her name is Gladys Nebbs."

Capri gasped. "She's his wife?"

"Yes. She's what carney folks call a stick. She starts the crowd. She's the come on. You'll find her still there at midnight losing a few quarters, winning a lot. You'd better learn all this before you put your foot into it. Haven't you worked in a carnival before?"

"No," said Capri promptly. And adding wrathfully, "Isn't there anything honest about a carnival?"

He smiled faintly at her indignation. "There's the merry-go-round," he pointed out. "And the whip, the Ferris wheel, the loop the loop, and the hooplas. And popcorn and ice cream and cotton candy machines."

Capri said suddenly, "How did Mr. Nebbs always make the wheel stop at his wife's number?"

"Oh, so you know about that," said Matt. He lowered his voice. "Well, in his case he controls it by pressure along the side of the table. It's called conducing. He leans against the table in just the right way. It's easier in closed-in booths; They just put their foot on the pedal under the counter."

"I think it's terrible," she said hotly.

Matt shrugged. "A lot of horse races used to be fixed, and maybe some still are. Ever seen a wrestling match?"

Capri nodded. "Once. With Uncle Shoe, in New York."

"Everybody knows they're fixed, most of 'em," Matt said, amused at her anger. "But the crowds eat them up. It's all fun, excitement, thrills."

"But—-"

"Look, kid," he said roughly, "everybody who stops at these booths, what do they want? They want something for nothing. They want to play a dime, a quarter, and win ten back. They're sucker bait, that's all. Why do they stop? Why don't they just keep on moving and stick to the rides? They're out for all they can get. Why blame the carnival?"

"You're defending them," said Capri.

He shrugged. "Why not? That's the way life is. If it's any different it's never given me a piece of it."

She watched him thoughtfully. "Just the same," she said, "my mother has her eye on some new attractions. There's a motorcycle troupe that she's telegraphing, and there's a man who dives one hundred feet into a tank of water."

Matt took her arm with something akin to excitement. "Is she getting him?" he demanded.

Capri shook her head. The indifferent air which he usually wore had completely vanished, and she wondered why. It seemed to have something to do with the man who leaped from the hundred-foot tower. Now he drew in a deep breath. "Maybe I'll plan to stick around and see what happens, after all. Maybe I was wrong about—-"

"About what?" asked Capri, smiling.

He flushed. "Well, about your mother."

"Why, what did you think of her?"

He moved his hands and made a curiously helpless gesture, as though he had not meant to be so blunt but must explain at once his indiscretion. "She used to be Francia Abbott, didn't she? You see, my dad has talked about her."

"Your father knew her? When? Where?"

"Your mother wouldn't remember. They played together in the same show at the Palace many times," Matt said. "Only my father started the bill. He was an acrobat. And your mother and your uncle had star billing."

"Well, for goodness sakes," cried Capri, radiant. "Your father was in vaudeville! Where is he now?"

He sounded angry. "Chicago. When things got tough on the circuit, he was one of the lucky ones. He dug ditches for awhile. Now he's a night watchman."

"Oh," said Capri, sobered. "I'm sorry."

"That's show business." Matt shrugged. "I guess acrobats are a dime a dozen, anyway. That's why *I'm* here."

She caught her breath. "You're going to be an acrobat, too!"

He nodded; then he smiled. It was the first time Capri had seen him smile; it transformed him completely, softening the angry line of his brow, making him younger and more vulnerable. "But right now," he said, "I've hired out my muscles so I can eat regularly."

They stood there smiling somewhat shyly at one another, realizing that they might be friends. Then Matt's gaze clouded; he straightened his big shoulders and scowled. "I'd better be running along," he said.

"Must you?" said Capri impulsively.

His lips thinned. "Look," he said, "I shouldn't have spoken to you in the first place. You don't want to know me. I'm just a roustabout." His mouth curled. "Roustabouts never talk to *people.* Didn't you hear what Doc Boone told you?"

"Doc?" faltered Capri.

"Sure, I heard him on the midway. And you did, too. He said it loud enough for me to hear, don't worry. He's got no use for me. He thinks I'm no good. Well, maybe he's right."

Capri stiffened. "I've never heard such ridiculous talk in all my life," she flung at him. "I certainly have the right to speak to whom I please, don't I? Well, don't I?"

He shrugged. "I wouldn't know," he said indifferently.

"Well, I have. Nobody can stop me."

It was like hurling feathers at a brick wall, he seemed so big and so impassive, but Capri thought that his eyes flickered queerly, as though he were moved. "I promised Jack a turn at his booth," he said. "I'll be going." But he added, hesitantly, "Honest I did."

She watched him thread his way through the crowd with the same light, graceful stride. Then Capri picked her way back through the sawdust and went into Madame Zela's tent only to learn that she must beware of a tall, blonde young man and all ocean travel.

CHAPTER EIGHT

Capri arose at ten o'clock the next morning, aware that this was a scandalously early hour for carny folk. Therefore, it was with some surprise that she saw Doc Boone walking swiftly up the hill from the carnival. She had just finished her glass of milk when he knocked at the door.

"Who in the world is that?" asked Francia from her desk.

"It's Doc Boone. Looks as though you'll have to meet him now," said Capri, with a glint of amusement.

"'Morning, Capri," said Doc. "I've got to see your mother right away." He was slightly out of breath from the speed with which he negotiated the hill.

"What is it?" Asked Francia, coming out to see him.

"How do you do, Mrs. Maccomb." Doc tipped his cap and took a deep breath. "There's been some trouble," he said.

"Nothing serious," he added, at the look that came over Capri's face. "One of the trucks caught fire."

Francia sat down. "Tell me about it," she said. "It's all right now?"

He nodded. "It was a near thing, though. I just happened to wake early and roll up a shade to see what the weather was like. It's a habit I've gotten into since we came here, carnies being so dependent on good weather. Well, I saw smoke drifting over the edge of the hill. You can be sure I'd jumped for my clothes."

Francia smiled faintly. "That was good of you. I'll go down immediately. Was much damage done?"

Doc shook his head. "I can repair it in one afternoon, easily."

Francia continued to stare at him; it was obvious to both of them that he was not finished. At last Doc cleared his throat and blurted out, "I think the fire was set."

"Set!" echoed Capri, sitting up straight.

He turned to her gratefully. "That's right. I'm almost sure it was done deliberately."

"That's nonsense," cried Francia. "You've nothing to base it on. Have you?"

"It's the way the fire burned," Doc said stubbornly. "It's spread out, lots of little fires springing up as soon as one was put out. And I got to thinkin'—-"

'What, Doc?" asked Capri.

He flushed. "I got to thinkin' how it was late last night that your dismissals were given out, the slips of paper telling a lot of folks this was their last week with Toby Brothers. I saw Mr. Sabo passing them out. It upset a good many people."

"Fran," cried Capri, "did you know about that?"

"Of course. I wrote them out myself. Sit down, Mr. Boone," she begged. And turning to Capri, she said excitedly, "Darling, I was keeping it for you today as a surprise. The Captain Southland motor troupe is joining us *next week*!"

"Say, now, I've heard of them," said Doc.

"That's wonderful, Fran."

Francia nodded. "And you should have seen the expression on Mr. Sabo's face when I told him." To Doc she said quickly, smiling, "Mr. Sabo had many doubts as to our success. But Capri, there's more."

"What?"

Francia beamed. "I've made inquiries. You remember that our next stop is Oak Hills? Well..." She leaned forward in a conspiratorial manner, her eyes dancing. "I just happened to know that there's a carnival lot empty next week at Canada City."

Capri's mouth dropped open in utter surprise; even Doc looked moved.

Francia nodded gloatingly. "If the show is cleaned up, they'll let us in. Just think of it, darling, a big city!"

Doc said uneasily, aren't you moving too fast, Mrs. Maccomb? This is a pretty small carny."

Francia shook her head. "We have to act fast, before we go bankrupt." She stood up and, in her excitement, began pacing the room. "You don't understand, Mr. Boone. Capri and I are sinking every hope into this carnival. It's all we have. When the season closes in November, we've got to have enough money for the winter, until the carnival opens again in March. I've got to be bold; we've got to be ambitious. We could lose the carnival so easily! You know the money is in the big cities, not in the small towns Mr. Sabo was content with." She halted, and said at last, defiantly, "And someday I want this carnival to be named Abbott and Maccomb. That's how good and honest it must be."

Doc shook his head. "You may not make it."

Francia looked surprised. "Why, we must."

Doc smiled and stood up. "Well, count on me," he said, sticking out his big hand. "And there's Ma, too. She'll certainly be pleased. And as for me, all I can say is that it'll be nice to be with a carny that's headed up for a change. Just bear that in mind."

"I will," said Francia and shook his hand. "I'm grateful."

"Now about the fire," suggested Doc, "will you be making inquiries?"

"Oh, no. I'm sure you're wrong in your suspicions. No, that won't be necessary, Mr. Boone."

"But, Fran," broke in Capri.

Francia shook her head. "No, really, darling. I'll just ask Mr. Sabo to keep an eye out at closing time. A cigarette tossed carelessly in the grass -—We'll think no more about it."

"Then I'll be going," said Doc. And with a kindly smile for Capri he opened the door and was gone.

"I believe I'll go down and see," Capri said, but Francia had already disappeared with excitement into the office.

Down at the carnival the crimson truck was scarcely crimson any longer; of the sign on its side that had advertised the Toby Brothers Traveling Show only a blurred T remained. Capri found it difficult to believe that in a few hours the truck might be restored to its former gaiety.

"Hello," said a voice from beyond the truck. "Guess we're the only people up and out of bed this morning."

Capri turned. She recognized the man standing behind the counter of the cat rack booth; she had passed him several times the previous evening and Ma Boone said his name was Archie. He was an amiable fellow with black hair which he frankly dyed and then plastered with brilliantine; his face was pink and leathery and long-jawed. He concealed his age remarkably well; Ma said he was almost 60 years old.

As Capri walked around the truck and approached him, he said, "What happened to that truck?"

"Fire. Doc put it out. You're Mr. Archie Lurch, aren't you?"

"That's right. You're the girl with the odd name."

"It's Capri," she told him.

He nodded. "Scarcely worth memorizing, though, since I'll be gone next week; but it's a pert name."

Capri glanced beyond him to the pyramid of balls that were stacked tidily on the counter; to the rear barely visible in the shadows, set the row of stuffed cats at which a player aimed.

At her questioning look Archie Lurch smiled. "No, there's no wheel connected to my game, but its none too honest. Person hits a couple of cats and knocks 'em over and I press a button here, so, and a gadget back there braces up the rest of the animals. You're welcome to go back and look but I can promise you'd have to sit on the cats to tip them over."

"Oh, I see," said Capri.

"I got the note from your ma last night," he went on briskly, and I'll admit it's just what I deserved. Only been in this business a month, and I don't like the feel of it. Your ma's only trying to get ahead; women always want to clean a place up when they first move in. She doesn't want any two-bit folks like me around."

"But what will you do?" asked Capri.

"Listen," he said firmly. "I'll get along. For instance, how old do I look, young lady?"

"About forty," lied Capri valiantly.

He nodded, pleased. "Plenty of jobs for a forty-year-old man."

"But what?" persisted Capri.

He shrugged. "Got a little magic act," he said. "Got pretty far with it once, but the younger boys passed me by, and I'm not had the chance to learn the new ways. I'm what you might call old fashioned, know what I mean?" He winked and then sighed, staring at his long fingers. "Maybe," he said hopefully, "maybe there'll be a place for me somewhere."

Capri wondered. "Show me a magic act," she suggested. "Please. I've never seen one."

He sighed. "But you know 'em. Everybody knows 'em. They even sell 'em in stores now for the kids." He said bitterly, "The coin that vanishes, the hat with an egg in it. And then, of course, the lady you saw in half. They don't sell that in stores," he added with a flash of humor.

"Let me see just one," she begged.

"Well—-" Archie turned his back. When he again faced her he bowed deeply and assumed a professional stance. Taking a handkerchief firmly in both hands he began tearing it into pieces. "My best one, too," he said brightly, "and all for you." Then he tossed the shreds into the air and caught them as they drifted down like snowflakes, stuffing them into his clenched fist. Gradually, secretively, he pried open his hands to reveal its emptiness.

"Now behold," he cried, clicking his heels, "it is one handkerchief again. And I draw it from the *other* hand."

"Wonderful," cried Capri. "How did you do it?"

He started laughing. "Excuse me," he said, and turning his back again she saw that the shredded handkerchief was dripping from his other sleeve she joined his laughter.

"You had two handkerchiefs," she cried, with mock indignation.

"It should be done with suitable equipment, and an armband worn above the waist," he explained. "My technique is a bit rusty."

"But it was fun," said Capri.

"Anyone could do that trick. It belongs to the amateurs." Archie's face clouded. "I dare say I do now, too. That's what they'll tell me. Well, that's life." He turned away and began dusting the radios, dolls, and cigarette lighters on the shelf behind him, the prizes that nobody ever won -—or ever could.

Just the same, reflected Capri, walking aimlessly on, it seemed as though Francia ought to know about this. Something might be salvaged. With all the strong games disappearing next week and only the hanky-pankys left the carnival midway promised to look empty and forlorn.

"If only," thought Capri crossly, "if only Francia would come down and meet some of these people."

It did not seem fair; what was it Francia had told Mr Callandar when she made her choice? "It's my world," she had said.

"Well, it isn't," Capri said aloud, scuffing the sawdust furiously and kicking an empty crackerjack box out of her way. "She's not really trying to make it her world. She just stays in the trailer all day and figures and figures. She's *afraid* to be friendly."

Perhaps the carnival reminded her dimly of the old days in vaudeville. Or perhaps it was too great a contrast to all the glamour that Francia had known. After all, Fran had once met the King and Queen of England. She must have known dukes and duchesses, too. Certainly, her beauty had been legend. "I made them laugh," Uncle Shoe had said more than once, "but your mother made them sigh, she was that lovely."

No, Francia wasn't used to shabby little carnivals run by people who wore tasteless, gaudy costumes, and lived on their wits alone.

"When Francia was in vaudeville," she thought dreamily, "she wore white all the time, white and gold, that's what Uncle Shoe said. Their acts were dazzling; everything was first rate. Even the scenery cost hundreds of dollars."

Sighing, Capri wandered into the shade of Mr. Sabo's deserted merry-go-round and sat astride one of the horses. With clear eyes she looked about her and saw the peeling paint and smelled last night's popcorn.

Uncle Shoe would have adored this, she thought. And with a start she realized, I do, too.

She had been so lonely until now, lonely all her life despite Uncle Shoe and Francia's closeness. But they, for all of their understanding, were adults and it had been their very closeness, their protecting attitude, that had kept her from knowing many girls of her own age. The carnival filled this lack. She loved its noises, its nightly crowds of townspeople, the grinder shouting at crowds in their hoarse, queer voices, the openers giving their set spiels, and over all the turbulence and glamour of fun-hungry townies enjoying themselves at the top of their lungs.

With a shuddering start the merry-go-round on which she sat began to move; The calliope began its wheezy, stomping rendition of a long-forgotten tune. Matt Lincoln stuck his head out from behind the machinery.

"Want a ride?" he shouted.

She nodded, smiling, and as the merry-go-round gained speed she blew the hair out of her eyes and settled back; her big yellow horse was a fast one, and as it plummeted her up and down she wanted to lift up her voice and sing, she wanted to do something violent to match the thrill of the music and the breeze tugging at her hair.

Matt climbed on the platform and mounted an adjoining horse. He, too, had caught the mood; they rode around without speaking, the music thumping gaily over their heads. They were Arabs astride fierce stallions riding over the desert into the sunrise, they were cowboys halting a stampede, explorers galloping recklessly towards the unknown. They were—-"

"Here, here," shouted Mr. Sabo, "what's going on?"

"Climb up," cried Capri, "we're riding to Singapore."

"Singapore or no Singapore," he said, "I've got to sweep the floor before the show. Be a couple of nice youngsters and vamoose."

Matt, who did not fancy being called a youngster, gave him a reproachful look. They dismounted and strolled together into the sunshine.

"I like Mr. Sabo now," confided Capri. "I didn't at first, but he's been very nice to Francia since she said he could stay on."

Matt said slowly, "He can afford to be nice."

She glanced at him curiously. "How old are you, Matt?"

"Eighteen."

"How long have you been with the carnival?"

"Oh, since March. Carny season starts in March. I graduated from school in February and hit the road South. Joined the show in Alabama."

Well, that was making headway, she thought. "Don't you miss Chicago?"

He stopped walking and faced her. "Chicago? I've never been to Chicago."

"Never? But I thought -—You said your father lived there."

He shook his head. "So he does. But I come from Albany. I was brought up by an aunt."

"What happened to your mother?"

"Oh, she is in Texas," he said, and began walking, his eyes on the ground, his hands in his pockets.

Capri tried to sort this out sensibly but gave up. "Matt," she said, "do you know anything about Archie's magic tricks?"

"Sure, but he was fired last night, I hear."

"Yes. But I was wondering—-" she wrinkled her brow and added vaguely, "he seems awfully nice."

"He is. I've seen the tricks. He used to be pretty good, I guess."

"What I was thinking was this," said Capri slowly. "Most of the children who come to our carnival haven't seen many magicians. They don't care how brilliant the shows are in New York or-or Chicago. Magic is magic to them."

Matt stared at her curiously, "Go on," he said.

She turned and faced him. "Why couldn't Toby Brothers Traveling Show have a magician? Archie's good. He looks wonderful to me. If to me, why not to everybody else who comes here?"

"What does your mother say to that?"

Capri chose her words carefully. "She doesn't know Archie. It wouldn't cost much, and it would give him a job. He's not as young as the others."

"You mean your mother might not like your having so much to do with carny folks." His voice was gentle.

"Oh Matt," she said fiercely, "I love it here. I do, I do!"

His lips trembled and then broke into a smile; it was so unexpected that it took her aback; He reached out and teasingly roughed up her hair. "I think it would be a wonderful idea, Capri; Honest I do."

"And you'd help if Fran says yes?"

She was surprised at the feeling behind his reply. "I'd be grateful if you'd let me," he said sincerely.

"Let him what?" said a friendly voice behind them, and turning they saw Doc smiling at them.

"Why, we're going to ask for a magic show," said Capri.

"The two of you?" Doc glanced quickly at Matt.

"The two of us," said Capri, "and you're wrong not to like Matt, Doc. He's awfully nice."

Doc grinned. "I was thinking myself that I might have been a little hasty." He put out his big hand. "Shake?"

Matt gave him a searching look. "I'm still a roustabout," he said.

Doc shrugged. "And I still don't trust roustabouts. Wouldn't trust one from here to there, but that doesn't mean I wasn't one myself once."

"You? A roustabout?" gasped Matt.

"Sure. Haven't I got enough muscle to pull ropes with the rest of you? Now are you going to shake this hand, Matt, or shall I put it back in my pocket?"

Matt laughed. "Put it here," he said, and they wrung each other's hands.

"My advice to you," Doc said, "is to stop bein' a roustabout soon as you can."

"I intend to," said Matt.

"Good," Doc bent and picked a long blade of grass, stuck it in his mouth and sauntered off. They watched him until he vanished into the Bingo tent.

"He's a good guy," Matt said.

Capri laughed. "You sound surprised."

"I think I am," he said, with an air of wonder.

CHAPTER NINE

"Fran," said Capri casually, after their early dinner, "it's my carnival, too, isn't it? I mean ‑—Uncle Shoe had us both in mind, didn't he?"

"Of course, darling," Fran said. "You're my daughter, aren't you?"

Capri nodded. The dishes were stacked clean and shining in the cabinet, and there was not much to hold Francia; in a moment she would be leaving for one of her interminable walks.

"Well, what I mean," said Capri desperately, "is could I, sort of as a hobby, try out an idea I've got?"

Francia looked quickly. "You don't mean down *there*, at the carnival?"

Capri nodded anxiously. "It isn't a bad idea. I'd like to surprise you. And you know how deserted the midway is going to look next week with all the grifters gone."

Francia winced. "Where do you pick up such language?"

Capri grinned. "You'd find it a lot easier if you spoke it, too."

Francia stood up and began pacing the room. "Capri," she said, "you aren't becoming too friendly with the people down there, are you?"

"I think they're wonderful."

Francia seemed worried. "Well, it won't be for long and, goodness knows, you *are* fifteen. I tried to remember that at your age I was already on the stage, but you seem so young."

Capri laughed. "I'll bet your mother said the same thing to you."

Francia smiled. "As a matter of fact, she did, darling." She sighed. "Well, what was it you were asking?"

"Just if I might try out a show. As long as it didn't cost too much money," she added swiftly.

"All right. Of course, you can. Play around with any ideas you want. Have fun." And, pulling on her sweater, Francia tucked up her hair and walked to the door. "Want to come along, Capri? I'm walking to the beach."

Capri lowered her eyes. "No, thanks, Fran. I thought I'd look in on Mrs. Boone." When Francia had gone she stirred guiltily. Once Upon a time it had been enough to accompany Fran anywhere she went; now she could not bear to be separated from the sounds of the carnival, whereas Francia wanted only to get away from them.

Capri ran to the closet and climbed into her dungarees and oldest shirt. She braided her hair tightly and plucking a scarlet sweater from the shelf she ran out of the trailer and down the hill.

Inside Madam Zela's tent it had begun to grow stuffy and airless. Too many people had come and gone. Even the playing cards were limp.

"But it's the kind of night that draws 'em," said Ma Boone, scurrying about in the rear of the tent to make herself a quick cup of tea. "There!" Carrying her cup and saucer, she sang deeply into the only comfortable chair, and taking advantage of Capri's visit began to greedily sip the steaming drink. "Nobody complains but me," she added cheerfully. "I'm getting' old."

"I don't believe it," grinned Capri.

"Get along with you," snorted Ma. "You been listenin' to that son of mine. Yes sir," she said, bringing out her feet from under the billowing folds of her gown and propping them on a stool, "they come from miles around. There's thunder in the air."

"I hope not. It's bad for business."

Ma Boone eyed her thoughtfully over the rim of her cup. "Mr. Sabo was in tonight," she said at last. "He seemed mighty unstrung about your ma's plans to take the carny to Canada City."

"It's our big chance," explained Capri.

"But Mr. Sabo claims it's a mistake. Does it strike you as bein' a mistake, Capri?"

Capri shook her head, wondering what was on Ma's mind.

"Butter wouldn't melt in that man's mouth lately," said Ma Boone slowly, narrowing her eyes. "He's certainly tryin' hard to be teacher's pet. Oh, well," she said, brightening, "tain't none of my business. Now you take the old days—-." She frowned and cocked her ear attentively. "What in tarnation's all that noise?"

Capri jumped up and ran to the door. Ma hobbled after her cautiously. The noise seemed to be coming from a small crowd several tents away; the group was rapidly swelling, the people on the outside craning their necks to see what went on at the nucleus.

"Come on, dearie," said Ma Boone, "it's another one of *them.*"

They fled down the midway toward the commotion. With Ma's awe-inspiring costume as a password, they elbowed their way into the center of the throng. Immediately, they found that Mr. Sabo had preceded them and was facing an outraged gentleman from the tourist colony.

"I tell you, my good man," boomed the stranger, "my wallet, my money, my keys -—they've vanished. You run a crooked show, sir. My pocket has been picked."

"I tell you, sir," said Mr. Sabo suavely, "we cannot be responsible for everybody who buys a ticket to our show. Pickpockets can get in here just as easily as you, sir. This is a decent, honest -—"

"I shall call a policeman," shouted the man. "I shall -—"

"Run and bring my mother," cried Capri to one of the small children who watched the scene. "Hurry, too."

"And who is this?" cried the aggrieved gentleman, turning.

"That's the owner's daughter," broke in Mr. Sabo, with a smile for Capri.

"Well, well," murmured the gentleman, but his eyes were fixed on the point beyond capri's head. She turned to see

Francia, who had just returned from her walk, hurrying through the circle.

"Doc told me," she gasped, out of breath, and then, swallowing hard, she said more calmly, "I wonder if you'd be so kind as to step to a quieter place, sir. I'm the owner and manager of the Toby Brothers Show."

"Why, yes, I'd be delighted," said the gentleman. "Indeed, yes." He was taking in Fran's shiny blonde hair, the purple scarf tied like a ribbon around her head. Capri smiled; it had been years since Francia had left vaudeville; it had undoubtedly been years since she had been stared at with such admiration. Do her good, she thought roguishly.

"Mr. Sabo, will you kindly come with us to the office?"

Mr. Sabo bowed deeply. "I'd be glad to," he said smoothly.

Capri turned away. The crowd was dissolving but it was plain to see that the bloom of the evening had worn off for them; there was a great deal of snapping of purses and wallets as everyone made sure that they, too, were not victims. A few headed for the exits. Jack Last gave her an impudent smile and left in the wake of an elderly couple.

"Well," said Ma Boone, "I hope your ma knows how to handle his type, but I dare say she'll give Nick Sabo a few lessons in honesty. Me, I'd kick that man out of the gate and tell him he ought to know better than bring a lot of money to a place like this."

"What do you mean a place like this?" demanded Capri.

"Now, now, dearie," said Ma gently, "I like your spirit. We both live here. I guess I can call it anything I like, but you know it's home to me."

"I'm sorry," Capri said in a low voice. Ma pinched her arm affectionately and went back to her tent to finish her tea before it became cold.

Matt was running the Ferris wheel. When he saw her, he beckoned to her. "What was all the shouting about?" he asked.

"A man got his pockets picked, Matt. At least he said so. He was mad as a hornet and it was awful; Fran has him up at the office now. Why, what's the matter, Matt?"

His lips thinned into an ugly line. "Darn it," he cried explosively, "I told him to lay off. I warned him. Why, the -—"

"You told who? What is it, Matt?"

"Nothing. Never mind. Here, hold this lever a minute, will you? I'll be back." And, to Capri's astonishment, Matt vanished before she even realized that it was her hand that now guided the Ferris wheel's turning. She was astonished. What was she to do now? Where had Matt gone, dashing off so impetuously?

"Joe," she cried desperately, "Joe, come here quickly."

Joe was selling tickets for the next ride. He looked up and paled. "Good grief," he shouted, "what are you doing with that lever? Give it to me."

He shot from his booth like a bullet from a gun. "Where's Matt? Who does he think he is?"

"I don't know. I'll find him," she promised, and left Joe gritting his teeth. But Matt was nowhere to be seen. She at last enlisted the aid of a man in the cookhouse and sent him back to sell tickets for Joe. Then she sped to the trailer, raced through the galley, and came to a discreet halt at the site of Doc, Mr. Sabo, and the stranger reposing comfortably on Fran's office chairs.

"This is my address," the gentleman was saying. "I live directly across the lake. Although I have no hopes of it being returned."

"Nor do I," said Fran regretfully.

"I'm only sorry that I upset you, Miss Abbott -—that is, Mrs. Macomb," he shook his head. "Just fancy my meeting you again after all these years."

"You know each other?" asked Capri, taken aback.

The gentleman beamed upon Francia like a father. "Certainly, young lady. Chrome's my name. I have your mother's autograph tucked away somewhere; with a rose she threw from the stage that I was fortunate enough to catch." He smiled. "Almost broke my leg catching it. And now I've got a son that same age and what is he interested in? Bebop! This generation has no soul." He plucked his hat from the desk. "Well, I must be going, but I hope -—that is, would you take it amiss, as an old widower like myself calling on you sometime for auld lang syne?"

Francia's face softened. "Thank you, Mr. Chrome. You're very understanding. And I'd be delighted to see you." For a moment she hesitated, and then she said quickly, "I'll show you out."

Mr. Chrome smiled. "I should go home, but I'm tempted to return to a certain booth and recoup my losses. A remarkable game: one throws a ball at the stuffed Adolf Hitler, a most pleasant pastime, but my pitching seems to have deteriorated."

"If I were you," said Capri firmly, "I would go home."

"Or visit us next week in Canada City," suggested Fran. "That would be Jack Last's booth, Mr. Chrome. He's been advised not to travel with us."

Behind her Mr. Sabo made a quick gesture. "I wanted to discuss that with you, Mrs. Macomb. That is, Jack has not been fired."

Francia turned. "Really? But I included him very definitely and asked you to take care of it."

Mr. Sabo coughed delicately, "Well -—that is, the boy is more than willing to make certain, er, adjustments in the game. He seems most eager to remain."

"You mean he's going to turn honest?" stated Capri clearly.

Mr. Sabo gave her a speculative glance. "Yes. And I am prepared to keep an eye on him."

"We can talk about this later," Francia said, looking dubious. "But, of course, if you are quite sure—-"

They had reached the front door of the trailer; Mr. Chrome shook hands with Francia. "It's been most interesting meeting your troupe. I'll say goodnight now."

"Just -—just a minute," said a queerly distorted voice from the darkness. It was Matt Lincoln leaning weakly against the side of the trailer, his chest heaving, his breath spent. There was a smear of blood on his forehead and his lips were swollen and out of shape. One eye was rapidly closing, the other glittered dangerously.

"Matt!" cried Capri, jumping down the steps and running to him. Mr. Chrome leaped to help her; together they tried to hold him upright.

"It's all right," mumbled Matt, trying to grin. "Just -—had a little -—fight."

"Yes, yes," cried Mr. Chrome, "but are you all right?"

Matt gasped. "Here's your money," His arm held out a leather wallet. It slipped to the grass and Doc picked it up.

"Who is he?" Francia asked softly of Mr. Sabo.

Mr. Sabo's lips curled. "Matt Lincoln. He works for you. And I dare say he stole it himself, the young beggar."

"Mr. Sabo, how could you!" cried Capri. "Can't you see he's brought it back?"

Fran said crisply, "Did you steal Mr. Chrome's wallet, Matt?"

"Oh, for goodness' sakes," snapped Capri, "we've got to have some bandages. Can't you find some, Fran?"

Francia ran into the galley and came back with a basin of water and a piece of clean rag. "Who did it, Matt?" she asked. "You must tell us. You're among friends."

From Matt's bitter glance it appeared that he did not share her confidence. His gaze slid across Francia to Capri, and then to Mr. Sabo -—there it caught and held.

"Yes, who did this?" asked Capri. "Please tell us, Matt."

Mr. Sabo lean forward. Matt moistened his lips.

"I'm no squealer," he said, staring directly at Mr. Sabo. "Find out for yourself. You've got the money back."

Mr. Sabo sighed deeply and managed to brief smile. "There's your answer," he said. "It looks as though that's all we shall ever know."

Mr. Chrome smiled. "But it should be very easy to determine the guilty party," he said. "I should say our young hero here got the better of the deal. He won the fight. Just look for another black eye. Perhaps," he suggested, "an even blacker eye."

Francia laughed. "Just the thing!"

But in the morning there was no need to look, for they discovered that Jack Last had, like the Arabs, silently folded his tent and stolen away. They never saw him again.

CHAPTER TEN

Archie was hunched dejectedly over his stall, his eyes staring blindly at the afternoon crowds that passed him by. He was nibbling absently on a blade of grass and even the artificial carnation which he always sported in his buttonhole looked limp and weary. At the sight of Capri and Matt, he brightened, but almost immediately his spirit sagged again.

"Archie," announced Capri, "I've brought Matt to see some more of your magic tricks."

"Now, now," he said, and hated her for mentioning them. All afternoon he had been thinking about them, remembering the feel of an audience, their bated breath, their cries of delight. It was all behind him now, and he knew it.

"Show us just one," she begged.

"Equipment's all stored in Newark, New Jersey," he said tiredly. "Need a lot of equipment."

"Well, show us a simple trick," suggested Matt.

Archie's glance came to rest on Matt. "Better put a steak over that eye," he suggested, and having made this much conversation he abruptly came to life. Bringing a package of matches from his pockets he tore off two and began playing with them, directing Capri to watch closely. It was like a juggling performance. Using the same easy, swift motions he suddenly found three matches in one hand, then six, then the entire packet.

"I don't get it," Matt said, frowning. "Where do they come from?"

Archie grinned. "It's all in what you think you see." He held up his hands. There, tucked between the fleshy part of his thumb and the curve of his palm were hidden an entire assortment of matches, ready to be shown at the proper moment or to vanish at will.

"You did it so quickly," breathe Capri.

Archie winked. "Practice. That's what you call palming. All it takes is know-how. I practice all the time to keep my hand in."

Matt looks steadily and affirmatively at Capri. She took a deep breath. "Archie," she began, "we have a proposition to make you. How would you like a magic show right here in this carnival?"

Archie turned pale. "Me?"

"You could have the big tent, the one the dancing girls vacate on Friday night. We'll build benches and use the bally platform as the stage. The children would love it."

Archie shook his head as though to clear it. "You want me as a magician?" He hesitated. "Your mother wants me?"

"My mother," said Capri, "has given me permission to try an idea of my own. She doesn't know yet what it is. Oh, Archie, please trust us; I know it's just a trial, but won't you take it on?"

A radiance like the rising sun spread over Archie's long tight face. "You don't have to argue with me, Capri. Why, I considered it a vast honor to stay."

"You'll do it?"

He said firmly, "I will write Newark, New Jersey, this very minute. Oh, my dear, the equipment I have there! The best of it, of course, was, unfortunately, pawned years ago. But I believe—-"

He stared into the darkness, planning it, wondering what was left.

"You be thinking," Capri said. "Tomorrow morning will go over every act you have. We'll weed them out. We'll find you costumes. We'll—-"

"Thank you," said Archie. And, drawing himself up proudly, he said, "Thank you. Yes. Indeed, yes, thank you."

"Come on, Capri," said Matt, and they withdrew, every bit as excited as Archie When they had checked over the big tent a second time, they were still so full of glee at a show of their own that they rode the Ferris wheel five times before Capri went home for luncheon.

In the morning, Capri, taking a running jump from the trailer to the grass, almost overturned Mr. Chrome who stood upon their doorstep with the canoe paddle in one hand and sunglasses in the other.

"Why, hello," she said. "I'm sorry."

"Not at all," replied Mr. Chrome admiringly. "Wish I could leave as spryly as that."

"Fran's in the office adding up bills if you want her."

Mr. Chrome coughed self-consciously. "Not entirely," he said. "I came also to invite you to a party."

"A party!"

"Er, yes. I have a son, you know, about your age. He's been wanting a dance." Mr. Chrome paused, and then with superb innocence put his foot into it. "When I was chatting the other night with your mother, she thought you'd love to come."

So Francia was behind this. "When is it?" Capri asked cautiously.

"Saturday night."

"Oh, I couldn't come Saturday night," Capri said with relief. "That's when my new show opens. Naturally, I couldn't miss it."

"Uh, no, no, of course not," replied Mr. Chrome, confused.

"We're rehearsing it now," went on Capri. "Just go through that door and you'll find Francia."

"Yes, of course," said Mr. Chrome unhappily.

He went in, and Capri stood a moment watching him go. She hoped the matter of the dance invitation would be dropped now; neither he nor Francia would understand her reluctance, but then, they didn't know.

As she walked slowly down the hill she was remembering that other dance, her very first, that she had not quite safely forgotten yet. The whole affair had been Francia's idea. Capri had gone faithfully to dancing class for many years, but not to the local classes where she might have made friends -—instead, every Friday afternoon after school, Francia had put her aboard the bus to Canada City where she might learn not only ballroom dance but tap and ballet.

"It doesn't matter whether you have talent," Francia had said. "Two theatricals in the family are enough, anyway. But it'll give you poise. You live such a quiet life with us both, darling."

But in the spring, Uncle Shoe had arranged a second talk between them. "It's the money," he had explained. "I know your mother wants only the best for you, but if we could transfer you to the River Junction Academy -—it's so much cheaper than Canada City."

"Oh, goodness," Capri had said with relief, "I'd much prefer the local classes. Why, I go to school with those people. It'll be so nice to know somebody."

The local academy for dancing was an academy in name only. Its classes were held over the Elks' auditorium in a stuffy loft full of broken-down chairs and an upright piano. Capri was transferred there just in time for their annual dance, and for this gala affair there was a new dress made by Francia and a corsage of sweet peas from Uncle Shoe. Capri had been terribly excited; it had never occurred to her that the few friends she had made in school might resent the fact that she was never allowed to play with them.

Capri would never forget the dreadfulness of the occasion, the rustle of the palms behind which the tiny orchestra scraped and played, and the cruel whispers of the boys and the stag line. "My father delivers milk at their place and *he* says nothing's too good for them. They don't have a dime left, but just because they were big shots once they want nobody's company but their own.

Capri danced once and it was abominable, hideously stuck with her partner. After that, she remained gratefully along the wall. Uncle Shoe and Francia, certain that their darling needed only to appear to be welcomed, never guessed the anguished she had suffered. They never realized what a cruel harvest their love of privacy had reaped Capri. She never told them.

Now she could hear Francia telling Mr. Chrome, "It's exactly what Capri needs. The child has eyes for nothing but the carnival, and it worries me because, after all, a carnival is no place for a teen-age girl to learn the social graces. A party is just the thing. And, of course, it will give her poise."

There it was, and she supposed it was what every girl had to face -—the insidious, shadowy visions that her mother had for her, the dreams and the plans. Some mothers had it lightly, like an attack of measles, others experienced it deeply, but until a compromise was found it was awkward and difficult for everyone concerned.

Poise, thought Capri. If you said it over a dozen times, it made no sense at all and was a rather ugly word. Poise, poise, poise.

"How extraordinary," said Capri. And standing still she suddenly tilted her head back and laughed. The sun was warm and bright, so bright that it washed the tent tops with silver and made almost no shadows in the tall roughly cut grass. The sky stretched blue as far as the eye could see, but most of all Capri laughed because for the first time in her life she had work all her own to do.

CARNIVAL GYPSY

Down at the carnival Archie had spread out his wares on a soapbox and was patiently awaiting her arrival. Capri climbed on a pile of rope and beamed at him. "Go ahead," she said softly.

They were not without an audience. In the shade of the merry-go-round Doc and Matt and Vincey Nebbs were nailing boards and logs together to form crude benches, while in another corner Slim Geibel was expertly painting signs advertising Professor Archibald, the Wizard of Wizardry, and Professor Archie, the magic man. Slim was a Jack-of-all-trades; his mother was the fat lady with a big circus, and although Slim occasionally tried jobs elsewhere he always returned in the end to the carnivals. They were in his blood.

Now Archie was holding up a bottle filled with water, his deft hands tipping it, his mobile face vastly surprised as he held it upside down and the water remained in the corkless bottle without spilling a drop.

"That's awfully good," called Capri, and entered it into her small notebook.

"Do it again," suggested Doc, watching closely. "You certain there's no cover to that bottle?"

Very much the showman, Archie graciously handed it around for them to examine; they were awed and wholly baffled.

"Now we need a finale, a climax," decided Capri, reading off the list of tricks. "Something big and flashy to finish with."

"Very true, dearie," said Ma Boone, joining Capri on the coil of rope. "But somebody tell me before I burst how that man keeps the water in that bottle. Archie, tell me quick. That's an order, too; I'm three years older'n you."

Archie grinned at her slyly. "Now Ma, you don't look a bit older'n Capri here, and you act a lot younger. You know I can't tell you the trick; you ought to have more respect for my magic."

"Hmph," sniffed Ma, "I won't respect you nor your tricks till I see you saw ladies in half. But you can't do *that.*"

They all turned expectantly to Archie. He did not disappoint them. "Well, now ma'am," he said with mock humility, "that's one trick I might do for you." His eyes gleamed mirthfully. "On one condition."

"What?" they all chorused.

He grinned. "On condition that Ma's the lady I saw in two pieces."

Ma squirmed with delight. "Tarnation, but you're mean," she said. "What's the matter, Capri?"

"That's just the thing for the finale," cried Capri excitedly, "with Molly dressed in spangled tights." And that was how they hit upon the climax for Professor Archibald's Wizard of Wizardry Show.

Around the midway, in what had once been Jack Last's booth, Mr. Sabo said and listened to the sound of Capri's laughter with a thoughtful expression upon his face. He was not happy; what particularly distressed him was that at the moment things seemed to be going so well. The Maccombs were beginning to make friends, which was dangerous for him -—Mr. Sabo had never underestimated the value of friendships. But what was even worse was that if he did not succeed soon in discouraging them, they might well discover the enormous profits he had culled from the show and neglected to report, over a period of fifteen years, to its owner.

That must not be.

Calmly Mr. Sabo listened to the gay voices emanating from the vicinity of the merry-go-round, and calmly he reviewed the situation. The fire in the truck had been discovered too soon, he had been a fool to attempt anything in daylight. And on top of that failure, he had lost Jack Last and gained an enemy in Matt Lincoln. He had underestimated Matt -—the boy was either playing a deeper game or was completely honest. But no matter what had happened before, one thing was clear -—the Toby Brothers Traveling Show *must* go bankrupt and soon; and would, in fact, be wisest to bring about its ruin before reaching Canada City. This did not give him much time.

He smiled. If he succeeded really well enough, he might purchase the carnival for only a fraction of what he had offered before. That indeed would teach Francia Abbott Maccomb that women had no place in a business like this. Back would come the strong games, they'd return to playing the smallest towns where the local policeman could be persuaded more easily to look in another direction -—for a price, of course -—and where the danger cry of the carny pitchman, "Hey, rube!" rang out merrily and often to bring the roustabouts running with tent pegs and threats. That was the life, with the sucker-money rolling in.

The sunshine was warm on Mr. Sabo's round pink neck. He stirred and sighed a little. Sunshine was the best medicine in the world for carnivals, but this one needed a bit of rain.

CHAPTER ELEVEN

"Fran, said Capri, "I'm going into town with Doc, and Matt. Docs taking the truck in. You don't mind, do you?"

Francia swung around and smiled; She had been baking a pie and there was a smudge of flour across her cheek. "Are you asking me or telling me? You sound like a girl who needs money."

Capri nodded frankly. "It's the show, Fran. I -—I need thirty dollars to buy two costumes and equipment for Archie."

Francia did not immediately go to the little safe that was set into the wall. She sat down on a stool and idly swung a foot. She said casually, a little too brightly, "Mr. Chrone was here this morning."

"Yes, I know."

"He's giving a party Saturday night. He has a son just about your age. Mr. Chrome would like you to come."

"I can't go," Capri said firmly. "That's the night my show opens, Fran."

Francia nodded. "I know that Capri."

"Well?"

They stared at each other warily, like opponents in a ring. Then at last Francia smiled a trifle grimly. "I want you to go, Capri. I simply will not have you turning into a tomboy at your age. You slouch around in disreputable dungarees and speak a perfectly odious language. Your constant companion is a roustabout who wants nothing more than to be an acrobat."

Capri could not believe her ears. "Fran!" she cried. "How can you say the word acrobat so scornfully when you yourself were in vaudeville?"

Francia looked surprised, and then uncertain, "Well, I don't want my daughter in vaudeville," she said weakly.

"Wasn't it good enough for you?"

Francia stood up and began to pace about the room as she always did when she was disturbed. "No, it was not," she said fiercely. "It's no life for a woman. I never liked it, either Capri. It's time you knew that. Oh, I love the fame and the fortune but there was never any rest, any privacy. I never had any talent for it, darling, you must know that by now. I sang only tolerably well, and my dancing was wretched, but they liked me. I kept on for your uncle's sake and -—Oh yes, for the money. It was wonderful to be acclaimed by everyone, to be popular, to be cheered and loved. But there were months and months of living out of one suitcase, one trunk, snatching bites to eat on the train, never getting quite enough sleep. It was Shoe who loved it. Goodness, how he loved it. But I -—I hated it."

"Oh, Fran," whispered Capri.

She nodded angrily. "That's why I want so much for you, darling. All the things I'd have liked, I intend for you to have; a safe, quiet life, college, parties, nice young men. That's why we're here, to somehow wrest some security from this wretched carnival Shoe bought. Do you understand now? Do you understand why you must go to Mr. Chrome's party?"

"Yes, but, oh, Fran -—"

Her eyes narrowed. "You force me to say that I shall forbid your act unless you go to the party Saturday night."

Capri shook her head. "You don't have to bribe me," she said quietly, trying to sort out what Francia had said and make it seem true. "Of course, I'll go, Fran."

Francia walked over to the safe and brought out the box of money. There, she said, counting the bills. "Thirty dollars, darling, and thanks. The dance is at eight o'clock."

Capri said softly, Fran -—Fran, I'm sorry. I wish you'd told me sooner."

Their fingers met and held for a moment. "You were always so proud of me," sighed Francia. "I hated to disillusion you, darling. Now run along into town and have a good time."

Capri hesitated, Fran said, "There's Doc tooting for you now. You'd better hurry."

With a little sigh Capri flung her arms briefly around Francia, kissed her, and then ran from the trailer. All the way into town she was silent, trying to absorb this new knowledge about her mother who had been so beautiful, but who had found no interest in the life that it brought her. But no matter how deeply sorry Capri felt, a tantalizing little thought crept stubbornly into her brain. *Oh, how I would have loved that sort of life!*

Matt said shyly," Would you like an ice cream soda, Capri?"

They had already made one trip back to the truck with an enormous load of packages; now they carried only a few in their arms. It was a warm, breezeless day with the heat plucking at the long line of mountains like violin strings, making them shimmer faintly to the eye. Doc had left them long ago for a junk pile that delighted him, and where he believed he might find something called a volt regulator.

"I'd love one!" exclaimed Capri, and they dipped under a cool awning into the dark interior of a drug store. But when Matt led her to a booth instead of a stool at the fountain, she turned crimson.

He grinned, "You're blushing!"

She admitted it. "It's like -—like a date, sitting at a booth," and adding in a low, apologetic voice, "I've never had a date."

"Are you kidding? Cute girl like you?" It was obvious he didn't believe her.

She shook her head. "I guess it's strange to you, but at the farm there were only the three of us. We always did things together. You know, picnics and hikes and trips into town. Once a year at Christmas time we always went to New York. We stayed a week and saw all the shows, and Uncle Shoe visited his old friends. And the agents, too." She smiled. "I think he always hoped for another comeback. Like Al Jolson, you know."

"You must have gone to school with kids," said Matt. And, as the counterman approached, he added with authority, "Two sodas, please."

"Strawberry," said Capri.

"Chocolate," said Matt.

"I went to a tiny country school," Capri explained, wanting him to understand. "There were ten grades and only two teachers. It was very small, and there weren't many students, either. There was a boy and another girl in my grade. The boy was awful, but the girl—-" her voice trailed away. She would have liked to invite the girl to the farm, but she had always been afraid that Fran might make fun of her; She was stout and freckled, her name was Griselda, and she knew how to do all kinds of things that Capri admired.

"For goodness' sake," said Matt, "how did you ever happen to be brought up like that?"

"Oh, that's the way it is in the deep, deep country," smiled Capri. "And then, Fran and Uncle Shoe being show people made our neighbors think we were a little queer. When nobody called at first Fran and Uncle Shoe got used to making up their own parties for me." She stopped and asked shyly, "When did you stop living with your parents?"

He said cheerfully, "When they busted up. My mother's married again and has three children. My father has two by his second wife."

"Oh!" Her heart sank, knowing how dreadful that must have been for him. "Was your aunt nice?"

He made a face. "Nice enough. But I'm sure she never misses me. I just decided to leave, that's all. And then Jack Last got me in here."

"Jack Last," she repeated.

He nodded. "He's as crooked as a pretzel, you know. He used to try to get me to help him."

She bit her lip trying to hold back the words that wanted to be said. They spilled out breathlessly. "Did you help him, Matt?"

He gave her a level, honest scrutiny. "I don't mind telling you that I was thinking about it. I got so I just didn't care. Nobody seemed to care about *me*. And then I told him I wouldn't, but I still didn't do anything about his being dishonest. Until suddenly I had to. Because of the carnival."

She nodded, her eyes shining. "You were wonderful, Matt, fighting him like that and bringing back Mr. Chrome's wallet."

"Drink up your soda," Matt said with a little smile. "I've owed you more than that for a long while."

She smiled. "Why?"

"On account of how it's your doings that I didn't fall in with Jack's plans." He glanced at her thoughtfully. "You're a nice kid, Capri. You didn't have to make friends with me. Nobody else did. You made me want to go back to practicing again."

"Practicing?"

He nodded. "You're making an awful racket with those straws," he teased. "Sure, I've been practicing every day at the lake. I've been learning to dive one hundred-ten feet into the water." He grinned. "Care to hire me?"

She laughed, but at his first words a little song had sprung up like a breeze in her heart. She was thinking. He likes me, he likes me. I've made my first very own friend.

"You can't be serious," she said.

"But I am. I think I could be a really fine acrobat; I know my dad was. But acrobats are a dime a dozen, and a fella has to start big -—it's the only way to get attention."

"Oh, but, Matt, diving one hundred and ten feet! And anyway, vaudevilles dead. What would you gain?"

He said seriously, "Vaudeville isn't dead, Capri. All over the country there are shows being put on in neighborhood theaters. There are night clubs, there's the circus and movies and television. And you've heard that vaudevilles back at the old Palace in New York."

She shivered a little, "I think we'd better find Doc. It must be time to go back." And she stared at Matt with dread, wondering how anyone could dream of danger with such wistful, purposeful eyes.

CHAPTER TWELVE

Saturday dawned with a vigorous west wind that swept away the low-lying cumulus clouds and left the sky an empty shining blue. It had rained the evening before. The dancing girls, all except Molly, had packed their suitcases and boarded the last bus for Albany. With them had gone the men who ran the wheels of fortune, the roll-down and ring games, the slum skillo, cat rack and three-card monte rackets. Only the hanky-panky's remained -—the penny arcade, the bingo tent, the penny-pitching board and the snake show. The gaps that were left in the midway would later be filled by the motorcycle thrill rides and by a tattooed lady that Doc had recommended. But it was sad, nevertheless, and Molly had wept to see so many go.

Capri had found a costume for Archie that she was certain would meet Fran's approval. It was a white tuxedo which they discovered in a secondhand store on their trip into town. Ma Boone had taken one look at their purchase and gone home to fashion him a sash and bow tie out of gold silk. Archie appeared unbelievably distinguished in it, and was thinking of letting his hair grow back into its natural color, which was as white as a suit.

There was also a table for Archie with any number of false bottoms that defied detection, and from Newark, New Jersey, there had arrived an assortment of carafes, ropes, velvet drapes and gaudy boxes. Under the makeshift spotlight, the stage, with its clutter of draperies and glittering objects, was blossoming into a garden of color.

All afternoon they work, the tent flaps closed to the handful of merrymakers that peopled the grounds. The benches were being set up, the microphone connected, and on the stage Molly was to be sawed in half. It was rehearsal time.

Capri did not as yet understand, but she was deeply excited at being promised the secret. "How can it be done?" she asked again and again of Doc. There were present only those who were to be in the act but it was surprising how many people were necessary to persuade the audience that Molly was, indeed, to be sawed in two. There was Matt, who was to be planted in the audience and invited on-stage to inspect the trappings; there was Archie and Molly and a thin young girl called Gracie who sometimes tended the popcorn machine when her husband had an evening off. At the moment Professor Archibald seemed principally interested in whether Gracie's black pumps exactly match the shoes that Molly wore.

"Why is she here?" Capri whispered to Doc." Why must their feet match?"

"Why," said Doc," she's in the act, too. Only the audience never sees anything but her feet."

Capri was thunderstruck. "You mean there are two girls? That's how it's done?"

"You didn't actually believe Molly was sawed into sections, did you?" grinned Doc.

"But where does Gracie hide?"

"Watch and see," counseled Doc. "Take a guess."

Capri leaned forward, her chin on her hands. She knew that a trap door had been cut in the stage but, on the other hand, there was absolutely no way to use it because Molly's box had been placed in the very center of a portable platform which was wheeled on stage at this moment, and which resembled nothing so much as a low billiard table set on legs and casters. It was well off the floor. There was not the slightest hiding place available for Gracie, and Capri told Doc so.

"Why?" asked Doc.

Capri explained, "The trapdoor is out because it's in plain view of the audience. In fact, the portable platform stands several feet above it; as for the boxes into which Molly will crawl, anyone could see their empty."

Doc nodded. "But that's magic," he said. "You're so impressed with the trapdoor not being used; you're overlooking the obvious."

"But what is it?" begged Capri.

"Why, Gracie's going to hide in the portable platform, the second one."

Capri gasped. "But it's too thin and narrow to hold a person!"

Doc grunted. "That's what you think. It's built to give just that illusion."

And, indeed, Professor Archibald was showing Gracie how to slide head first through a tiny hinge aperture in the floor of the portable platform. When at last she had disappeared, Capri found it easy to forget about her completely.

"Okay, Molly," said Archie. "You know your part."

Quietly Molly laid down in the long gaudy box, placing her hands and feet through the wooden stocks at each end.

"Only those are Gracie's feet and Molly's hands and head," chuckled Doc. "Molly's cuddled up in only half of the box, while Gracie has slid her feet up through the trap door. Now watch this. Archie sauce a box in half, and look—-"

Capri laughed. It was perfect. There stood Archie between the two boxes. Molly's lower limbs were completely removed from her head and enjoyed a separate life of their own.

"Now when I suggested," ordered Archie, you flutter your hands, Molly, and you wiggle your feet, Gracie. Can't have the audience thinking we've got a dummy in there. Give Gracie a tap in case she doesn't hear."

Gracie apparently heard; the feet moved and rhythm with the disembodied hands. The illusion was uncanny.

"Okay," called Archie, "now we'll try the finish. Do it all backwards. I slide the boxes together; Matt helps me wheel the platform around. That's to prove there's no trickery, you see. But while it's being done, Gracie, you sneak your feet back in and, Molly, you lie out straight and substitute your feet so that when the box is opened you're lying there just like you've been pasted back into one piece again."

They accomplished it with exquisite precision. If Gracie's feet were withdrawn at the proper moment Capri had no way of seeing, but when the box was at last open wide there was Molly, with no hint of a second pair of legs nearby.

"Oh, Doc," Capri cried when he joined them, "it's positively thrilling. Do you think Archie would teach me a few -—just a few tricks?"

Doc smiled and pinched her arm. "I kind of reckon Archie'd be pleased to teach you all of 'em," he said, "seeing as how you've given him his chance. Isn't that right, Matt?"

But Capri had not waited for Matt's reply. She had disappeared backstage to learn more secrets. When she emerged again at the end of the afternoon there was something not quite the same about her. In an indefinable way she had changed.

"This is for you," Francia said, her eyes shining over a long cardboard box. "Capri, I bought it for you in town this afternoon. It's for the party tonight."

Capri glanced up from the arduous task of pulling on nylon stockings. Her mind had been filled with thousands of busy thoughts; the method of palming, of holding an audience through sheer talk, the principles of magic, the thrill of her first lesson. She looked up to see Francia holding a mass of cloud-like material in her arms.

"Oh, drat it," she said good naturedly, "you mean it's *that* kind of party?"

"Of course, darling. It's a dance. You know, soft lights, dreamy music."

Yes, and dances with countless young men, thought Capri grimly; well, that was something Francia would never see. She fastened the dress and stared sadly at her reflection in the mirror. She looked wonderful.

"Do you like it?" Fran asked at last.

"It's gorgeous," Capri said politely.

"It is on you," Francia said softly. She stood up. "I'll go and see if doc has the car ready. He'll come for you, too, at midnight."

Alone, Capri fussed helplessly with the dress; she was pleased and curiously excited at the reflection in the glass. But the evening ahead depressed her —she would have given anything to remain and see Archie and Molly give their very first show.

She moved, and the reflection in the mirror moved, too, trailing misty white chiffon behind it. "I'm in white," thought Capri, "just the way Fran was in white once."

But Francia had always worn touches of gold with her costumes. With a snap of her fingers Capri whirled about in the center of the room and came to an abrupt standstill. Then, running to Francia's trunk, she tossed aside shoes and blankets until her fingers at last touched France jewel box. Yes, it was still there. Reverently, Capri brought it out —a heavy necklace of imitation gold, almost as wide as her arm and, yes, here were the matching bracelets. Capri had not seen them since she played masquerade in them as a child. Swiftly she secured them about her throat and wrists and turned to find the mirror again.

There she was. She leaned closer. She looked different, older, lovelier. Almost unconsciously she curtsied and swung into a caricature of a tango. An unseen audience held its breath in wonder as --—she smiled at her absurdity --—as she carelessly changed pace and would supple fingers wrought new miracles in magic. To her ears came the applause of thousands.

"Bravo! Bravo! Encore!"

"Capri," called Francia from outside, "we're waiting. Do hurry!"

"I'm coming," replied Capri, but she did not move. In that second, she knew what her heart had been telling her for days and what her mind had only now grasped --—the carnival, vaudeville, all the show business in the world was in her blood. There was far more of Uncle Shoe than of Francia in her. It was like quicksilver streaming through her veins. That was why the carnival was a home to her as it could never be for Francia. This was her first taste of it, but she knew that it was only the beginning. Whatever came of this moment there could never be anything but the stage for her.

"Capri," called Francia impatiently.

With quick fingers Capri unfastened the gold necklace and the matching bracelets. She did not need them now. She left them lying on the bed like a vivid promise.

CHAPTER THIRTEEN

Mr. Chrome's summer cottage was a credit to his architect's good taste and to Mr. Chrome's sizable bank account. It hung over the lake like a fragile pink shell; there was a terrace upon which, for the party, were hung dozens of papered lanterns and there was a small orchestra sitting precariously at the foot of the rock garden. But for Capri it was a nightmare almost from the start, for it was apparent at once that this was to be her second debacle.

It was the sort of party where everyone knew one another from other summers and shared a great many hilarious experiences to which they referred without preamble. "Do you remember at the creek?" one would shout as they sat in the long living room, and this set them into peals of laughter. Or, "D'ye remember Marty? What a card!" And for Capri, whose life had included neither Marty nor the creek, it became more and more difficult to laugh.

Mr. Chrome's son Peter was a tall, bony fellow with kind eyes and a carefree smile. There was a whole assortment of other boys who were equally as carefree and kind, but their kindness did not include Capri, who, when the dancing started, stood alone under the orange and blue lights and tried to make herself as small as possible. The sudden elation before her mirror had died to a faint pulsebeat. This was another evening to be endured rather than enjoyed.

There was a girl named Linda and a girl called Kitty. There were others, but these two were the ones to watch; they swung lazily over the floor with the continuous line of dance partners, they called everyone by nickname as softly and frequently as possible, and they parried witticisms like queens.

Standing in the shadow of the grape arbor someone accidentally bumped against Capri; she turned and gave the boy a too-bright smile, and was ashamed as she saw him back hurriedly away as though he were afraid she might insinuate herself into a conversation with him. It was because she was new and strange, and an unknown quantity, she told herself -—but she had always been new and strange except at the carnival.

She retreated to a chair and sat down, removing, as though it had been pinned on, the smile that said to everyone, isn't it a grand party? I'm having a wonderful time, whatever made you think I wasn't?

It was a smile that she had not meant to wear, but it was automatic, like the peculiar vivacity people adopt when talking to strange elderly ladies in churches or railroad stations. The world of the carnival was a thousand miles away despite the fact that she had only to raise her eyes to see the spotlights painting the sky along the north shore.

"Would you care to dance?"

Capri glanced up in surprise. A carrot-haired boy of twelve or thirteen stood blushingly before her. Somewhere behind the chair in which she sat there came to her ears a faint giggle, which led Capri to guess that Carrot Top was carrying out a dare.

"Why, I'd love to," she said, and moved into his arms defiantly. It was a matter of infinite relief to be removed from that one spot along the wall.

"I -—I don't know as I've seen you around before," began the boy resolutely. "You here for the summer?" (And like an undercurrent, "Step together step, step together *step*.")

"No, you haven't seen me before," smiled Capri. "But we're leaving Sunday, anyway."

The boy threw someone an agonized glance over her shoulder. "That's tough," he said, stepping on her toes. "You got a nice tan, though. Where you been staying?"

Capri took a deep breath. "At the carnival," she said dazzlingly. "Have you visited us yet?"

This confused Carrot Top so completely for a moment that he stepped on both her toes. "What do you mean 'at' the carnival?" he asked. "How can you stay *at* a carnival?"

"Why," she smiled brightly, "it's very simple. We own the carnival. It's ours, my mother's and mine. We live there in a trailer."

Carrot Top stood stock-still in the middle of the floor, oblivious of the hazard it caused. His face registered shock, then consternation. "Have you been in jail?"

Capri laughed. "No. But all afternoon I've been watching a girl sawed in two."

His jaw dropped. "I don't believe it!" He grasped her arm and pulled her into a sheltering corner. "How's it done?" His fierce, snub-nose face peered up at her demandingly.

"That wouldn't be fair," she said.

"I'll bet you don't know. You're just kidding."

"I do so know. For that matter, I'm going to be a magician myself."

There was now mixed with Carrot Top's expression a distinct look of awe. "Do you know any tricks?" he asked. "Any that you can do?"

"Do you have a package of matches?"

"Why, sure," he said happily, "I got some in my pockets from lighting the lanterns. Here."

Capri took them. Please, please, she silently prayed, please make this work. Cautiously, slowly -—but her audience was inexperienced -—she did Archie's trick of making the matches appear and disappear in her hands.

"Boy, oh boy, that's neat," said Carrot Top. "Can you do any others?"

She thought a moment. "You wait here," she ordered, "I'll be back."

In the Chrome's living room she found what she needed, and reappeared only to find, to her surprise, that Carrot Top had gathered a larger audience for her.

"I got some of my friends," volunteered Carrot Top. "Give 'em the works."

Neatly copying Professor Archibald, Capri filled the soda bottle with water, fingered it hopefully and turned it upside down. It worked. Not a drop escaped.

"Wow," shouted Carrot Top and, in his enthusiasm, did a war whoop. The orchestra ground to a startled pause; two dozen pairs of eyes swiveled mercilessly to the door where Carrot Top's special friends clustered around Capri.

"What's up, kids?" asked Peter Chrome pleasantly.

"Look," said Carrot Top with feeling, and pointed at the bottle that Capri still held. "Now do the match tricks. C'mon."

"Oh, no," protested Capri, wanting to sink through the floor.

"Oh, yes. Please," said Peter Chrome, and left Kitty standing in the middle of the floor to watch.

There followed a dizzying few minutes which for Capri were as magic as the tricks she displayed with increasing skill. Without fanfare she was the attention of everyone and the hit of the party.

"She's got a magic show," cried Carrot Top. "Over at the carnival. It's all hers, too. They saw a lady in half. "

"Oh, how?" cried someone.

"She won't tell," Carrot Top informed them importantly.

"I've never seen that done," said Peter Chrome. "It must be something to watch."

"Let's make her tell," cried one of the younger boys, looking extraordinarily fierce.

"I've got a better idea," said Peter, looking at his watch. "Let's dance for half an hour more, and then all go over to the carnival."

"Splendid!" chorused everyone.

The orchestra burst into music again. Carrot Top moved aggressively forward, and this time there were no snickers from his confederates. "Dance with me?" he demanded, his chin up like a warrior.

"Sorry," said Peter Chrome, "she's going to dance with me. You've got to," he said apologetically, "I'm the host, only somewhere I'm mislaid my manners."

As they swung out onto the dance floor together, Capri's smile said to everybody, Isn't it a grand party? There was nothing forced about it now.

At ten o'clock three cars moved up to the entrance of the carnival to deposit a shouting confusion of young people in evening dress. "It's alright, Charlie," said Capri, running ahead to the ticket window. "They're my guests. We've come to see the magic show."

"You mean you brought the whole party with you?" gasped Charlie.

Capri nodded, her eyes shining. "They wanted to come. Honest."

Charlie scratched his ear thoughtfully. "Have to make you a grinder," he said dryly, "you must have given 'em quite a spiel."

"She did," said Peter Chrome. "I never saw a party dissolve faster."

As they filed through the gate, Capri felt a thrill of responsibility for the carnival and her show. The lights strung across the midway danced against the wind like giant fireflies; each booth was rosy with color and brightness. At the merry-go-round Mr. Sabo gave her a shout that was foghorn-sized; from Ma Boone she received an impudent wink.

"Your show's doin' all right," called Ma. "Been a line at the door all evening."

There was still a line. On the platform Slim Geibel was dressed in a star-and-stripe suit that came close, but not too close, to approximating Uncle Sam. "Hully, hully, hully," he was shouting in his enormous hoarse voice, "step right up for your tickets to Professor Archibald, the greatest, the incomparable———"As Capri passed him he bent down. "Well, well," he said, "why don't you bring this many people every night?"

"I'll try to," she said.

"Your mother went in just about three minutes ago. You could have knocked me over with a feather. And when she saw that it was a magic show you could have knocked her over with a feather. She sure looked queer when she read the signs."

"But she's still in there?"

"She ain't come out," said Slim succinctly. And straightening, "Hully, hully, hully, ladies and gentlemen, to see———"

The group hurried chatteringly down to the first row and, in the confusion of taking their seats, Capri turned and stole a glance at the back of the room. She was not certain how Francia would accept this newest development, the adjournment of the party to watch Molly sawed in two; she spied Francia at last in one of the side rows and waved. It was alright. Francia was smiling, her smile including the whole party.

Capri's glance fell away and with a little start she saw Matt sitting across the aisle. He was staring moodily at Peter Chrome, absorbing almost hungrily his fine clothes and confident, easy manner; then his gaze dropped to hers and there was something so vulnerable in that swift glance that Capri turned away. For that moment Matt's defenses were down and she could read all of the hurts that had ever scarred him, and it no longer seemed incomprehensible to her that he had not known which road to take. Then the lights in the tent flickered and died; Matt's face became only a pale blur, and the audience eagerly faced the stage. When the lights came on again three-quarters of an hour later Matt had disappeared.

"That was elegant," breathed Carrot Top in her ear, enjoying a certain proprietory feeling about the evening. "Do we get to meet the professor?'

"See, he's coming now," she said, "and, everybody, I'd like you to meet my mother, Francia."

They stood in a circle, all of them talking at once. "It was excellent," cried Francia. "My dear, you and the professor have seen to everything and, believe me, I know."

"Was it all right? Did it go off well?" cried Archie, rubbing his hands together.

Capri nodded. He had proved delightful; his drollery was amusing, his costume superb. It made her happy to realize that her contribution to their carnival had proved a success, even though she had been responsible for only the skeleton of the idea. Yet something was missing.

"Excuse me," she said. But no one noticed her run up the aisle and leave the tent. What she missed was Matt; he, too, had a stake in the magic show. He, too, ought to share in the gay remnants of praise. The hurt, defiant glance he had sent in her direction ought to be wiped out.

He should know they're only visitors, she thought. The carny belongs to us -—to Matt and me, and Doc and Ma Boone, and Slim and Mr. Sabo and Francia.

But Matt was nowhere to be seen. She looked among the Ferris wheel carts and the prancing merry-go-round horses. Nor was he in the cookhouse or at Vincie Nebbs' booth or any of the other concessionaires'. She stood at last on tiptoe and searched the faces of the dwindling crowds. That was how she came to see what no one else had noticed yet.

A cloud of smoke was crawling idly up the seam of the magic tent that she had just left. It moved so listlessly that it seemed of no significance whatever; it was not unlike a vaporous snail weaving a path across the top of the tent, disappearing here to reappear there. As Capri watched, too astonished to wonder why it was there, a burst of black smoke suddenly joined it from the rear. The entire magic tent was on fire. A thin tall column of flame issued from the smoke and streamed heavenward, licking hungrily at the wires that reached tenuously toward the loop the loop. Capri screamed as the lights flickered and went out, leaving the carnival tangled in a black shroud.

CHAPTER FOURTEEN

There was no possible way of saving the magic tent. The fire leaped up to devour the canvas in a matter of seconds and like a gaudy animal crouched in readiness to spring elsewhere. From the throats of a hundred panic-stricken people came the ugly roar, "Fire! Let us out!

In their haste they overturned the popcorn wagon and left the gate and splinters. The tall canvas screens were trampled down as though a herd of cattle had stampeded across them. In the shouting crowds that pressed forward-looking for exits only a dozen people turned back to help.

Matt was suddenly among them to help Slim pull Francia and Archie from the magic tent. Together they struck the tents that surrounded the fire and tugged yards and yards of stubborn canvas out of its reach, isolating the greedy flames, giving them nothing new to feed upon. The nearest fire department was five miles away, but there was no time to search for a telephone. They were forced to rely on strangers to summon help.

The wind was their enemy. It had been blowing hard all evening, and now it was the chief peril. It sent shreds of burning carbon and live embers shooting into the sky like miniature fire puffs. What had once been one swollen fire now turned into a dozen small ones.

They worked in a dim twilight. Doc Boone climbed at once to the top of the Ferris wheel from which he could see the rooftops and shout directions.

"Fire on Ma's tent, Doc would shout from his lookout post. Then they would stream forward like an army ——a ridiculous army with weapons of dirt and sand, and brooms and sticks and hatchets.

"Fire on Nick Sabo's trailer roof," Doc cried. And the army would split into platoons and then into squadrons.

When the crimson fire trucks at last drew up to what had once been the carnival gates, Professor Archie's magic tent was only a heap of black ashes.

"Well," said Ma grimly, "that's that."

Capri gave her a quick glance. In her haste Ma had pulled on a pair of stiff dungarees and an old, ragged shirt of Doc's. Her face was smeared with dirt; she cradled an ax in her arms as though it were a baby; she looked exactly like a pioneer grandmother who had slain her first Indians and demanded more. Capri might have laughed if she was certain that her laugh would not turn into a sob. Instead, she groped wearily for the merry-go-round platform and sat down, resting her chin in her hands.

Francia said in a strangled voice, "How bad, Doc? We're not ruined, are we?"

"Now, now," Doc said soothingly, "you just relax and leave things to Nick and me. Everything's going to be all right."

"On the contrary," said Mr. Sabo giving Doc a reproachful glance. "Things look very bad, Ms. Maccomb. I don't want to sound pessimistic—-"

"You're not only pessimistic, you're wrong," Doc said curtly. "Take another look around, Nick. We've kept the damage down to the one tent and the canvas screens. What's so bad about that?"

Mr. Sabo gasped. "Why you must be mad. You saw how the fire spread. It was tremendous."

Doc shrugged, "Go look for yourself, Nick. The carny's lucky, that's all."

Francia said quietly, Thanks to you, Doc. If you hadn't pulled down the tents around the fire it would have spread in three seconds. That wind!" she shivered a little and wrapped her blackened sweater closer.

"I'll take a look around for myself," said Mr. Sabo stiffly and withdrew to join the firemen who were poking among the ruins.

"Doc", said Francia.

"Mmm?"

Her voice was very low. "How about -—that is, do you think—-" she bit her lip. "Doc, we're due in Canada City tomorrow."

Capri rose and stood beside Francia. Even Doc could see that Fran was going to cry. Getting the carny to Canada City meant too much to her. It had become an obsession.

"Why, I think we can manage," said Doc gently. "Supposing we move on tomorrow as planned. We'll work all night, that's the best hope, and finish up in Canada City. Yes, I think we can just about make it."

Francia drew a deep sigh of relief, "And now, ma'am," said Doc, "I'd suggest you run on back to the trailer and get some sleep. Nick and I can take over."

"I ought to stay," faltered Francia. "At least until the firemen leave."

"Let me, Fran," begged Capri. "Please."

"All right," Francia's smile ended with a tiny sob. She turned and, with Ma Boone on her arm, went back to the trailer.

"I guess I'd better run along too," said a voice behind her. Capri turned to find Peter Chrome at her elbow. She had forgotten all about him. "You're still here?" she said in surprise.

"Why, sure. Fire fighter Chrome, they call me." He grinned. "I must say you supplied us with more fireworks than we bargained for, didn't you?"

She laughed. "I'll say. Thanks for helping, Peter." she glanced over his shoulder and caught her breath. "Why, Matt," she said, "where have you been" I looked—"

Matt nodded. "I know. It was silly of me to run out on the magic show like that, but I -—I was angry. I went for a quick swim to work it off. I wish I hadn't. If I'd stayed around I might have seen the smoke before you did."

"The damage has turned out to be small, Matt, isn't that wonderful?"

"Excuse me," said Peter Chrome, "but I'd better be running along now. So long, Lincoln, it was nice meeting you."

Matt's hair was streaked with soot and his face was smeared with grease, but the flash of his smile as he grinned at Peter was warm and sincere. I'm glad you were here," he said.

Peter laughed. "I should be saying that," he told Capri. "In the middle of things I thought Matt was trying to smother me to death with a rug, but it turned out that my hair was on fire. He was the only one who seemed to notice."

They were still saying goodnight when the fire chief joined them, his face very stern.

"Where's Mrs. Maccomb?" he asked.

"She went to bed," said Capri. Can I help? My mother was so upset, we sent her home."

"You're her daughter?"

"Oh, yes."

Wordlessly the man held out to her a newspaper on which he had sifted several pieces of canvas. "See that?" he demanded.

"Yes. But what does it mean?"

He touched the fragments with a finger. This didn't burn," he said. It was blown away. But if you'd sniff it, you'd find it still reeks of kerosene. We've also found remnants of cloth in which the kerosene was originally dipped. Your tent was systematically fired by someone."

"Oh, you must be wrong!" cried Capri. "Why, who would do such a thing?"

The fire chief shook his head. "It was set. No fire ever started that fast without help. Now the point is," went on the man heavily, "what do you want me to do about it?"

"Why -—why, I don't know," faltered Capri. "That is, we're moving on to Canada City tomorrow morning. We've got to."

The fireman shrugged. "It's your funeral then. I've given you the facts, and I'll trust you to report this to your mother. Good night everybody."

They watched him stalk back to his men, converse a few minutes, and then return to the truck. Capri said in a low voice, "It couldn't be the grifters this time. They all left last night."

"Unless there should be one of them still hanging around," suggested Mr. Sabo anxiously, and emphasized his point by glancing stealthily behind him.

Doc angrily kicked a stone. "I don't like this," he said. "I don't like this at all."

Mr. Sabo said regretfully, his eyes on Capri, "This will upset your mother still more. It's deplorable."

"We don't have to tell her," she said thoughtfully. "At least for a few days, until she's gotten over the shock of this."

"A splendid idea," said Mr. Sabo.

Doc shook his head. "I've got a feeling she ought to know,"

"Monday," suggested Capri. "We'll tell her Monday. By then we'll be in Canada City and this will all seem like a bad dream."

They agreed to this and parted. But only Capri went to bed, and each time she awoke during the night to glance out the window, it warmed her heart to see the lights flashing along the midway like fireflies as Doc directed the men in making the repairs as swiftly as possible.

They had been singing all the way. From Slim's truck, where she was perched on the high front seat, Capri had grown used to the sound of the voices swelling loud only to die into whispers as the wind snatched them back. Gay songs they were, but now as they approached the new field in Canada City the gaiety changed to sadness.

"There's a long, long trail a-windin' into the land of my dreams."

Capri hugged her knees listening. The song caught at her throat as it always did, its ineffable sadness melting something close to her heart. She could hear Gladys Nebbs' voice above the others, and it was a surprisingly fine soprano, strong, confident and true. Her babies were asleep in the trailer behind her. Capri wondered whether she minded this nomadic gypsy life.

Aloud she said dreamily, "I used to see carnival trucks winding past our farm every spring and summer. They'd always pass very early in the morning, but I'd hear them. There was a window by my bed, and I'd sit there and wonder about the people and the wagons, whether they were happy or not, what kind of lives they lived."

"And what do you think now," asked Slim, his hands firm on the wheel.

She smiled. "I've never met any people quite like them."

"Perhaps you never will," said Slim as he slowed for a curve and checked the trailer behind them in the mirror. "I tell you -—a carny fellow has a call inside of him that's bigger than himself. He's always looking for something around the next corner, the next bend in the road. And he's chock full of tomfoolery and not quite real. Not according to your standards, anyway."

"What do you mean, my standards?"

Slim laughed. "You're used to three meals a day, aren't you? And a quiet life with eight hours' sleep. Give a carny man a dozen people and he's lonely for more. Give him four walls, and pretty soon he's putting a towrope and wheels on them and making a trailer. Yes, sir ,the carny man is the last frontier, the last gypsy left."

Capri set up straight, pleased. "Really gypsy?"

Slim nodded. "Oh, he doesn't wear rings in his ears -—not on the outside, anyway. But it's there, inside him, in his blood. There's nothing quite like it among the circus or vaudeville folks, though vaudeville folks come close."

"Why?" asked Capri, wide-eyed.

Slim grinned. "Because a carny man doesn't need talent to make him a carny man. He's just born a certain way and thinks of a gimmick to give him the life he wants. He lets people like your mother have the headaches of owning the rides and arrangin' things. He moves in and makes suckers out of the townies for thirty weeks of the year, and then he goes south for the winter, and somebody makes a sucker out of him in turn. And what a life!"

"But circus people—-." He shook his head. They're artists, craftsmen. And that's the way it is clear up to the top of the heap. He smiled. "The carny man's at the bottom and he knows it. But what does he care? He buys some flash -—the expensive items like radios; and a lot of slum -—that's what people win, the cheap stuff; he pays the carny owner a percentage of his take and gets fed and housed and taken care of and—-. "His smile deepened. "And there's always a rainbow around the next corner."

"Why do you stay?" asked Capri. "After all, you've worked everywhere and your mothers in the circus."

"Yep, I've got a foot in both worlds," admitted Slim. "But my tonsils like carny air best. I'm carny, that's all. Jack-of-all-trades, master of none. A rolling stone." He honked his horn gaily at a dog that ran across their path. "Your mother'll have her hands full keeping sharpers out of the show. There aren't many carnies that don't let the pitchman work strong, and the ones that don't are the big rich ones at the top. They can afford to keep 'em out."

"She's doing all right so far," Capri said.

He threw her a quick glance. "I wouldn't be too sure. And that's a word of warning. This was the second fire since she took over; some people are beginning to say your mother has us jinxed. They're saying that she's bad luck for Toby Brothers, and they're talking like they want Nick Sabo back."

"That's silly," Capri said shortly. 'We own the show, and he doesn't."

Slim shrugged. "That's what I hear, anyway."

They road on in silence through the noon-bright streets of Canada City. When they had left the tall buildings behind, Slim turned down a dusty macadam road and Capri saw the other trucks parked ahead.

"We're here," said Slim laconically. "This is it."

"This?" echoed Capri in surprise.

Slim sighed and stretched his long lanky legs. "Another day, another dollar. Getting' out?"

Capri obediently opened the door and jumped down. They were on the very outskirts of Canada City. Less than half a mile away a railroad track ran along a steep embankment, off to their right a factory spewed smoke into the air through tall chimneys. There was not a tree in sight, and, in the distance, the city dump smoked lazily in the sunshine. To their left, silhouetted against a gray sky, was the city itself. The wind made soft caressing sounds as it swept from the city through the acres and acres of grass that stretched level to Capris' eye. It was one of the most desolate wastes that she had ever seen.

"Going to miss the lake?" asked Matt, walking up to them.

"Miss it!" she wailed mournfully. "If we could only go back! I thought Canada City would be big and special."

"Well, it won't look so bad when the tents go up," said Matt. "I've seen worse. And when Captain Southland gets here with his motordrome, it'll fill up some of these wide-open spaces."

A long black sedan drove past them, kicking dust into their faces. Capri made a face.

"That's a police car," said Matt.

"Really?" They turned and watched as the car slowed to a stop. A tall thin gentleman emerged to accost Doc. They exchanged a few words, and Doc pointed; the man nodded and walked over to the trucks where Francia and Mr. Sabo were supervising the unloading.

Matt sighed. "That looks like the sheriff himself. They're sure careful. I guess Canada City means business."

"But so does Fran. Let's walk closer."

"Me? I'll bow out now. I've got to earn my keep." He grinned, and turning a full somersault came down squarely on his two feet and kept running. He vanished into the cookhouse."

Doc and Slim were examining the one damaged dynamo, mysteriously squinting and probing. Beyond them, Francia and the sheriff were having an animated discussion near the trailer. Capri wandered over and sat down on the steps, wondering what function was hers on moving day.

The sheriff's back was to her, but Francia seemed to be doing most of the talking, anyway. She was wearing a loose drab sweater today, and even baggier slacks. She made an amusing picture as she waved her arms angrily. Her voice was blown to Capri on the little gusts of wind that rippled the grass.

"I don't care what you've heard, you need have no qualms, whatsoever," she was saying. This carnival is not crooked. Maybe it was last week, maybe it was last year, but I'm in charge now. The Toby Brothers Traveling Show is not the biggest carnival in the country, nor is it the showiest, but I can assure you, sir, there are absolutely no wheel games here. I hope that you will inform this -—this committee for Better Government of yours that we are not hoodlums, but perfectly respectable business people.

"But my dear Mrs. Maccomb—-" began the sheriff.

"Never mind," said Francia stormily, "you have made your point quite clear. I trust I have made mine equally as clear."

The sheriff turned, with a little helpless gesture that seemed at once ironical and humorous. There was a trace of a smile at the corner of his mouth as though he were completely bewildered at the reason for Francia's vehemence. His glance felt absently too Capri, and then returned with interest.

"Why, hello," he said. "It's Capri, isn't it?"

Capri stared at him blankly for a moment and then guess. "Why Mr. Gayfeather", she cried.

His smile broadened; he seemed curiously excited. "But what in the world are you doing here? You and your mother drove out to watch?"

They shook hands cordially. "How is the farm?" Capri asked.

"Thriving, absolutely thriving," he said immediately. "And your mother, the gracious Francia? Is she in Canada city, too?" He hesitated, and then said shyly, "You see, I feel I know her quite well. Her portrait still hangs in my study I'd like very much to meet her."

Capri laughed. "But you just did. She's standing right behind you. Fran, this is Mr. Gayfeather who bought the farm from us."

Francia looked incredulous. "Not the gentleman who sent the flowers!" She flushed crimson and gave him an accusing glance. "You were a sheriff all the time?"

They both stared at one another so indignantly that Capri laughed. "But we were carnival owners all the time!"

It was Mr. Gayfeather who hastened to retrieve the situation. He bowed and smiled. "Do you dislike sheriffs so deeply, Mrs. Maccomb?"

Francia stiffened. "Do you distrust carnival managers so implicitly?" she inquired coldly. She put out her hand, Mr. Gayfeather grasped it briefly and, feeling that the amenities have been exchanged, Francia turned to Capri.

"There's a great deal for us to do now, darling. If Mr. Gayfeather will be so good as to excuse you?"

"But, of course," said Mr. Gayfeather. And with a bow and a quick look at Francia's scornful face he withdrew.

CHAPTER FIFTEEN

For Capri it was strange to watch the carnival spring up on a new field. There were the same carts, the same machines and tents, and booths, but their arrangement was ever so slightly different, like a paper tracing that had slipped a little to one side. To return to their trailer Capri had to check her first impulse toward the lake. There was no lake, nor were there trees or any kind of shade at all. The trailers lay behind the midway in a circle, partly for protection from any tramps along the railroad, and partly in a communal effort to break the full force of the sun. Awnings had blossomed immediately, and now when Ma Boone shelled peas on the steps of her trailer she sat under an umbrella.

On Monday morning Capri and Francia had hardly finished breakfast when there was a knock upon their door, scarcely heard above the din of the 9:00 o'clock news. Francia said grimly, "Darn it, my toast will get cold. Do butter it, will you, Capri?" She fretfully snatched open the door.

There was a faint admiring whistle. A strange voice said, good morning, darling. Capri was so startled that she left the toast and came to peer over Fran's shoulder.

"It's Captain Southland and his motordrome," explained the confident voice. "Now you wouldn't be Mrs. Maccomb?"

Capri's mouth dropped; she frankly stared. Captain Southland was small, fastidious and delicately fashioned. His hair was worn in a high pompadour, liberally oiled, and his full, petulant lips were pointed up by a pencil-line mustache. But he was no weakling. Beneath the silk jodhpurs and scarlet shirt, his muscles rippled like snakes slithering through the grass.

"I retract whatever recalcitrant remarks I espoused upon seeing your two-bit setup," he said gallantly. "With such a charming proprietress how can a man be so wrong?"

"Well," said Francia, thinking of nothing else to say, "you're here at last."

"Here, and ready to perform for you, Madam. Cap Southland at your service."

"Yes I see." Fran started to smile, bit her lips, and reconsidered. "Well supposing you park your trailer over there, Mr. Southland. We'll—-"

"But I have three trailers!" he cried, wounded. "See?" He pointed and they beheld a startling caravan of crimson trailers. Beside one of them posed a small, lissome brunette with waist-length black hair and lips so vivid, it seemed from a distance as though she must be holding a rose between her teeth.

"That is Felicity," commented Captain Southland tenderly. "Does she ride, too?"

"Gracious! Does she ride?" Which did not exactly answer the question but satisfied Captain Southland.

"Well," said Francia helplessly, "I'll round up some roustabouts and have them make room for you."

"Thank you, darling," said the captain, and strode off with a great display of shoulders, leaving Capri in a state of merriment.

"Laugh all you want," said Francia, smiling, "but we're paying a small fortune to bring him here." Capri sobered immediately.

The parking of the three trailers, emblazoned on every side with the captain's heroic deeds, was a long and arduous job. The erection of his portable Motordrome promised to fill the entire day for, beneath his florid exterior, Captain Southland was a perfectionist and at heart an economy-minded miser -—he wanted everything for nothing. At the sight of a scratch upon the red paint of a trailer he bellowed like an angry bull; upon seeing a motorcycle swung too recklessly from the truck, he was threatened with collapse. His temperament was exhausting. Capri soon tired of him and walked down the midway to visit Doc.

"They're here," she said. "He's big time all right, but what a vision!"

"I hear he acts like one, too," commented Doc. "Hand me that wrench, will you, Capri? Thanks. Now isn't it mean of me, talking behind a chap's back like this?" His eyes twinkled as another angry roar floated down the midway toward them. He said, "you wouldn't think such a little fellow could make that big a noise."

Capri flopped down beside him and hugged her knees ecstatically. "I don't want to interfere with your working but, oh, Doc, isn't it grand that we're here? I know the view isn't breathtaking but, just think, Canada City *is* the capital of the state. Imagine the people will get all week." Her eyes clouded. "But how I wish the tent hadn't burned. It would be so exciting to help Archie tonight."

Doc said, "it would be kind of exciting for Archie, too. But if business is good maybe your mother'll be able to buy another tent soon." He jerked his head in the direction of the Bingo tent. "Archie's in there. I've put him on the expense list as extra help."

Capri gave the Bingo tent a wistful glance. "What's he doing?"

"Patching canvas."

She sighed, and automatically began flexing her fingers.

"What's that for?" queried Doc, looking up.

"Magic. See?" She held out her hand. She had secured a package of matches between her fingers. "I'm practicing palming."

Doc grinned and went on insulating a wire. Capri's gaze moved around the midway. A few yards away Mr. Sabo was polishing the brasswork on his merry-go-round. As Capri watched, he took a cigar from his pocket, sat down in the swan boat, crossed his legs and relaxed. Catching her eye he gave her a genial smile. "All set for the big night?"

She nodded vigorously. "I'll say!"

"Yes, indeed," replied Mr. Sabo. "Looks as though your mother's troubles are over. Well, look over there! Here comes the sheriff."

Mr. Gayfeather was crossing the field carrying a bundle in his arms. As he passed the motordrome he nodded with polite interest to Captain Southland and continued his long stride down the midway. When he saw Capri there was no mistaking his look of pleasure.

"I came to see you," he said. He held out one hand, to Capri's surprise, he was carrying a bouquet of lilacs. They're past their height, and rather buggy," he admitted ruefully, "but they're from your farm."

"Your farm?" echoed Doc.

Capri glanced back and nodded. "Of course," she said. "That is, it used to be ours, it's Mr. Gayfeather's now. It's about seven miles outside of Canada city, in River Junction."

Well, I'll "be doggoned," said Doc, and watched her join Mr. Gayfeather and begin to stroll slowly towards the trailer.

Mr. Gayfeather was saying, "I didn't mean to interrupt your conversation. Nor did I plan to see your mother. I wanted to -—well, to explain something that troubled me."

"About yesterday?" asked Capri.

"About yesterday, I'm afraid -—that is, have I offended your mother?"

Capri smiled. "It's quite alright, Mr. Gayfeather. You were shocked, weren't you, at finding us running a carnival?"

Mr. Gayfeather looked at her with deep interest. "You thought that?"

She nodded. "I suppose," she admitted shyly, "you believed we were in anything but strait circumstances. I dare say you thought we were going away to live with the maiden aunt, or to the city where Fran would be starting a very exciting career."

Mr. Gayfeather smiled boyishly, "It did take me aback, but she is beginning a very exciting career. For me it was a great adventure, finding your farm for sale. An enchanting place, you know; the day I met the two of you and bought the farm will linger a long time in my memory."

"The two of us?" Capri frowned. "But you didn't meet Francia until yesterday."

A deep scarlet flushed Mr. Gayfeather's cheek and quickly disappeared. "You must forgive me; I met her portrait that day. That, of course, is what I meant."

"Do sit down on the trailer steps," suggested Capri. She dusted off the top step for him and they sat down. "Fran's off supervising Captain Southland with his motordrome, so we're quite alone."

She was not sure why she said this, but Mr. Gayfeather seemed relieved. He said, "I was wondering if the two of you would care to visit me at the farm next Sunday. I'd be happy to entertain you. As a sheriff your mother may very well think me a most unpleasant person, but I can assure you that I was not born a sheriff." His eyes were twinkling. "I am, in fact, a retired woolen manufacturer and, until being elected sheriff, I was quite a stranger to Canada City."

Capri smiled. "She did think you unpleasant, but I do believe it was because you didn't recognize her right away as the beautiful and gracious Francia Abbott."

"Aha," said Mr. Gayfeather, "that's just it. I put my foot into it, didn't I? I was afraid so. I have enjoyed her portrait so much." He grinned boyishly. "But you must admit the slacks were extremely baggy and she was wearing a delightful dab of mud across her cheek."

Behind them a board creaked. They both whirled. Francia said Furiously, "I didn't mean to eavesdrop. I came back for a drink of water. Mr. Gayfeather, I think you are the most odious, disagreeable, hateful person I have met in a long time. I am so sorry that the cut of my working clothes offends you, I'm not used to such elegant people. But never have I met such an insulting—-"

Mr. Gayfeather stood up. "My dear Mrs. Maccomb," he said, "I meant no insult. On the contrary I was only amused at my own stupidity."

"You have a very superior attitude," cried Francia, struggling for words. "It's quite obvious what you think of carnivals and -—and me. I find it very difficult to be civil to you."

She moved down the steps with the hauteur of a queen, glanced angrily at Mr. Gayfeather's outstretched hand, and then at Mr. Gayfeather himself. At the faint smile that she saw gathering in his eyes, she flung herself away from them and started running down the hill.

Mr. Gayfeather smiled ruefully. "My dear Capri," he said sadly, "I fear your mother doesn't like me."

"Well," said Capri frankly, "I guess you don't like her very much, either." And she wondered at the look of surprise that Mister Gayfeather turned upon her.

CHAPTER SIXTEEN

It was almost six o'clock. Doc walked out of his trailer, crammed on a battered felt hat, and walk down to the midway. Mr. Sabo emerged from the cookhouse sucking on a toothpick; he glanced first at the sky and then at Matt and Capri, nodded, murmured his greetings with customary courtesy, and went on. From the largest crimson trailer came Captain Southland, his mouth open in a yawn. "Hello, darling," he said to Capri." Just how much of an audience do you expect in this provincial town?"

"It's a city," said Capri tartly, "and you better hurry up. The window opens in ten minutes."

"Dear, dear," said captain Southland mockingly, and disappeared in the middle of his second yawn.

"What a guy," said Matt. "Gosh, when I'm that well-known just catch me acting like that, and you can give me a punch in the nose."

"I'd love to," smiled Capri. As they passed, Capri gave the Bingo tent a thump; it had been put up despite Canada City's outlawing of the game, but it was only for storage. "I hate to see it empty," sighed Capri, thinking of it. "There's almost room inside for a magic show."

"Better let well enough alone," advised Matt. "It's too small, anyway, and there's no stage."

They made a complete tour of inspection, pausing for a long time before the round motordrome. The building resembled a squat, fat oil tank, with an outside balcony from which the audience could watch the pit. The gay canvas roof held a flagpole from which fluttered the stars and stripes. Somewhere inside they heard the sudden burst of a motorcycle warming up.

"That would be Felicity," said Matt. "Doc says she's even better than the captain, but I'll bet *he* doesn't think so."

"Look," said Capri, "the gates are open. There's the first customer coming in! Where are you going to be tonight, Matt?"

"Ferris wheel again. And maybe I'd better get over there right now; those kids dashing in have Ferris wheel written all over them."

When Matt had gone, Capri looked around and spied Ma Boone lighting the lamps at the front of her tent. "He's a nice boy," said Ma, jerking her head towards the Ferris wheel. "You know what month he was born in, dearie?"

Capri did not.

"Well, he's a very nice boy but I'd better consult the charts before I say more. Bring him around sometime for a nice cup of tea, dearie. You ask him."

"His father was in vaudeville," volunteered Capri.

Ma looked her over shrewdly. "That makes him all right with you, eh? Yes, well I hear he plans to join it, too. Doc says he's a rare acrobat. You've only to see him to know."

"He practices a great deal."

"Yes, and I hear he's got his heart set on someday diving a hundred and ten feet into a tank of water."

"Oh, he'll never do that," said Capri.

Gradually the midway was filling up with people. The air was cluttered with gay balloons and toy canaries flying from the end of sticks; younger mouths were dripping with cotton candy and frozen custards. At seven-thirty the lights went on and, as the twilight deepened, the Ferris wheel turned into an enormous sparkling toy. The carnival's brightness made walls against the darkness and the line of cars along the road into Canada City became two and then three deep.

It was enough for Capri to watch the townies. They waited in line for their fortunes to be told by Madame Zela; they hung about the hanky-pankys, the run on pennies was phenomenal, and filled all the wagons for the rides. The carnival was small for such a crowd but, at the speed with which people flowed through the gate, Capri could see that with such great luck she and Fran might be adding new concessions and new rides before the season finished. It was a heady thought.

When Capri found Francia at last, she was on the steps of Captain Southland's Motordrome balcony. It was close to nine o'clock and Fran was jubilant.

"That show was worth every cent we put into it," said Francia. I finally stopped counting the crowds and came to watch the captain."

Capri could share her pleasure. She had been both awed and amused -—amused at Captain Southland's extravagant gestures, and awed by his breakneck daring. Inside that small circle Captain Southland had ridden around and around until his motorcycle had gained such speed that he jumped it to the wall and then, as everyone stiffened in horror, he had ridden horizontally around that wall and removed his hands from the handlebars. How he had lived so long Capri did not know, but she would not lightly mock him again.

"He's a real hit," Capri agreed.

Francia flushed with pride. It was good to see her on the midway. What did it matter if Fran saw in the carnival only the possibilities for money and more money, and ignored the romance that fired Capri? It was enough that they were both working towards the same end.

They walked together down the steps. "It's small, but it's an honest show now," Francia said. "The first extra money we have, I'll put Archie back to work, Capri. Perhaps we can add a headless girl to the snake show and a tattooed lady."

"How about a contortionist? And a House of Fun?"

They agreed the possibilities were endless. Farther down the midway they paused briefly at Vincie Nebb's new Spin-the-Arrow, a harmless game with a slum prize for every player. Somewhere to the west came the faint whale of a siren, and they stopped to listen.

Capri smile. "It sounds as though the mayor is coming. Hear it?"

Francia nodded. "I wondered if you did, too." As it grew louder, she put out a hand to Capri and stopped her. "What in the world is it?" she asked frowning.

It was such a raucous noise that others had stopped moving, too.

"It's an ambulance. Somebody's been hurt."

"No, it's not an ambulance," said Francia. She began running. Over at the gates Capri saw a score of heads swiveling towards the entrance; a few people hurried closer. Then the group around the gates drew back. Someone cried out and an ominous hush seemed to cover the carnival.

"What is it?" demanded Capri.

"Don't you know?" gasped the gentleman to her left. He turned and saw her. "You better run home quick, girlie. It's a raid. It's the police."

"A raid? Oh, that's impossible." But at the same time Capri found herself running to join Francia.

It was impossible to see, there were too many people, but as Capri threw herself into the crowd demanding an entrance, she suddenly bumped headlong into Francia and Mr. Gayfeather.

"Fran," she cried, "what is it?"

Francia was pale and furious; she seemed almost to be hanging upon Mr. Gayfeather's arm. "What is this all about?" she was crying. "What are you doing here with these -—these men? Why the sirens?"

Mr. Gayfeather's face was expressionless. He stopped and faced them resolutely. "I'm sorry," he said, "I'm extremely sorry. You must understand that I'm not in charge of this; I came along only to make it easier. Mrs. Maccomb, this is a police raid."

"A what? But I've told you," said Francia patiently, "there are no wheels allowed on these grounds."

"Who's this?" asked a policeman at his side.

Mr. Gayfeather's face softened a trifle. "This is the owner of the carnival, Dick. I'm sorry, Mrs. Maccomb, but we received a tip by telephone just fifteen minutes ago that you've been secretly carrying on gambling in one of your tents."

"Why, that's preposterous!" cried Francia.

Mr. Gayfeather nodded, gave her a courteous smile, and walked past her.

"Fran," said Capri, "let them look around. Don't lose your temper, you'll only—-"

"The idiots!" breathed Francia. "Why, they're ruining our first night here! Everything was going so well!"

But Capri was watching Mr. Gayfeather and his small retinue of men. They seemed to have no doubts about their destination -—they were headed straight for the empty Bingo tent. Very efficiently Mr. Gayfeather pulled back the flaps of the tent, and he and the men disappeared inside. Their shadows leaped crazily against the sides of the tent. That was when Capri first realized that a light had been burning inside.

Then Mr. gayfeather stepped out. His face was very stern. He gave Francia and Capri a curious look, as though he were measuring them, turning them inside and out. A regretful smile twisted his lips. "Mrs. Maccomb," he said.

"I hope you're satisfied now," said Francia. "Really!"

Mr. Gayfeather held open the tent flap, and something in his face made Capri look past him. She caught her breath in horror.

Where only that morning there had been piles of rope, chairs, tent pegs, and odds and ends of canvas, there now stood three wheels of fortune. Whoever had placed them there had gone to considerable care and expense for there was not a detail overlooked -—there was money lying carelessly about on the tables, and two chairs were overturned, as though at the sound of the sirens a dozen people had fled without regard to what they left behind them.

Capri heard a sudden intake of breath as Francia, too, looked inside. Then with a little whimper Francia collapsed, much like a puppet being tidily folded away, and Capri and Mr. Gayfeather caught her just in time.

CHAPTER SEVENTEEN

With a fluttering sigh Francia opened her eyes; they had placed her in Ma Boone's bunk and for a moment she struggled with the effort to recognize her whereabouts. Then she gave a little moan. "Oh, no," she whispered, "I remember now. But I can't believe it. I don't understand."

"You've been framed," Doc said, his hands on his hips. "You've been framed, Mrs. Maccomb."

"Framed," she echoed, and closed her eyes. "Capri, where's Capri?"

Capri came forward and placed one hand in Francia's. "Here I am, Fran," she said.

"How bad is it, darling?" asked Fran, and suddenly opened her eyes. "Tell me," she demanded. "I must know what happened. You're holding something back. What did that horrible Mr. Gayfeather do?"

"He's not really responsible," said Capri gently. "He came along only to try to prevent them from -—well, to make it easier for us. It's the Chief of Police who -—who—-"

"Who what?" Francia's voice was sharp.

"Now, now," said Ma Boone, separating them with an elbow. "Here, dearie, drink this. Have a sip of nice hot tea. You've had a bad shock, dearie."

"I don't want any." But as Francia opened her mouth to protest, Ma Boone serenely fed her a spoonful of tea. Francia sputtered, choked, and sank back.

"Try to sleep a little now," Capri begged.

Francia gave her a distraught look. "You think I'm going to sleep now? Tell me immediately what happened."

"Fran -—"

"Tell me."

Capri sighed; it was an order. "The Chief of Police -—well, he arrested some of us."

"Who?" demanded Francia.

"He arrested Matt, Vincie Nebbs, Charlie Marconi." A rueful smile played about her lips. "And Captain Southland and Felicity."

"Oh, no," whispered Francia. "How could they?"

But Capri nodded. "It was between their acts. You know how impudent Captain Southland can be."

It was Ma Boone who finished the summary. "There'll be a big fine, of course. But because of the Better Government League -—"she bit her lip angrily. "Because of them they're closing us down."

Francia set up straight, her eyes incredulous. "Closing us down!" She cried. "For the whole week?"

They nodded, not quite able to meet her eyes, knowing what a calamity this was. There was a long, long silence and then, without a word, Francia turned her face to the wall. "Go away," she said stiffly, "leave me alone."

"Fran -—"

"I said leave me alone. Please, Capri."

Capri followed Doc out the door, her eyes stony. They walked straight out of the trailer into a singing darkness.

"How is she?" inquired Mr. Sabo from the shadows.

Doc sighed. "I don't like to see a person crumple like that. I don't like to see hope drained out of a body like that. It's not right."

To Capri he said, "Ma will be there with her. Sometimes it's best not to have anybody who's too close at a time like this. Ma's tea will set her up in no time, that and Ma's talk." He touched the brim of his shapeless hat. "I'll go down now and spread the word around so there'll be no trouble when the police come back to close us down." He shook his head. "There'll be some folks quitting. I'm afraid."

Capri and Mr. Sabo watched him go. "Mr. Sabo," said Capri at last, in a low voice, "is it the end of the carnival?"

Mr. Sabo nodded. "I'm sorry, but it looks like it."

"But why?" cried Capri. The carny's still down there, nothing's changed. I don't understand."

"Well," said Mr. Sabo unctuously, "you're going to be fined. It should be quite a fine, too, because of the assurances your mother gave the Canada City authorities that no wheels were allowed. Then you have five people to be bailed out of jail.

Their fines will run from twenty-five to one hundred dollars apiece. And -—had enough?"

"No. Go on," she said bitterly.

"Then you're going to be closed down within the hour. Where will you go? Where can you reopen the carnival for the rest of the week? You can't stay here. They won't let you. The lot in Oak Hills has been taken. A carny like this has to bring in a couple of thousand dollars every week or it goes under. Your mother has no reserve funds. She's been working on a shoestring, counting on this week to set the carnival up for good. Well, there won't be any take this week. Your mother's trapped."

"Oh, Mr. Sabo," cried Capri. She sat down on the grass with a stunned thump. She had an overwhelming desire to cry, but the memory of Fran's white face forced her chin up. "Mr. Sabo, who can hate us so? Who could have played this dreadful prank on us?"

Mr. Sabo's voice was perfectly controlled, a combination of sympathy and regret. "I don't know. I couldn't even guess."

"Well, it was fiendish," said Capri. "And I'm not forgetting the fire in Cottsville, either."

"Fire?" said Mr. Sabo. "Why, yes, that's true." He sounded a bit uncomfortable.

"Well, Canada City can't do these things to us. I won't let them ruin our carnival -—not after all the hopes Fran had."

Mr. Sabo gave a short, ugly laugh. "But who's to stop them?"

Capri thought about this a moment. Friends? Francia had no friends except a few in New York who had known her years ago. There was Mr. Callandar -—but remembering his prim, disapproving face, she put that thought away immediately. People needed friends at a time like this; people to rally around and defend them; people to say, this is outrageous, Francia Abbott Maccomb doesn't have a dishonest bone in her body, she promptly pays all bills, she sends her daughter faithfully to Sunday school, she is kind, upright and honest, and completely without guile.

A sad little smile crossed Capri's face. For a lonely, heart-rending moment she realized where Francia's love of privacy had brought them. She realized it with a surge of anger that sprang up like a flame, anger because it was so unnecessary, because they were so close to River Junction and there ought to be someone to step forward and protest. Then, loving Francia, the flame died and Capri's heart swelled with forgiveness. Francia was Francia. There could be no blaming her for living her life the way she enjoyed it most.

"There must be some way," Capri said.

"There is." Mr. Sabo sat down in the grass beside her. "I'm going to help you and your mother."

"Really?' she breathed.

"Yes. "

"Oh, but how, Mr. Sabo?"

"I am going to take this carnival out of your hands."

"Oh," said Capri, her heart sinking.

"I've grown fond of you," went on Mr. Sabo in his courteous voice, "and, of course, I'm fond of the carnival. I've given most of my life to it. I don't want to see your mother go bankrupt and the carnival up for auction. I can speak to you frankly?"

"Yes," said Capri, sighing a little.

Mr. Sabo said kindly, "I have made your lawyer several propositions at various times. I am willing to make another offer. I will solve your problems for you and you can leave here, forgetting the whole misadventure."

For a moment Capri loathed him. Then, thinking of Francia, she said, "that's kind of you, I'm sure."

"Of course," he added, "I could offer only half the price that I offered before."

"Of course," agreed Capri quickly. It was wrong to hate him, he had been so very kind and now he was being even kinder. It was only that something would die a little inside her at leaving the carnival and going back to the same quiet, private life.

"But I could not let the offer run indefinitely," said Mr. Sabo. "You'll tell your mother this when she has recovered? Say tomorrow morning? I shall bring the papers for her to sign at two o'clock."

He seemed very sure of himself, thought Capri, but then, perhaps he should be. They had no other alternative.

"Just the same," said Capri, "I think I'll run into town in the morning and talk to Mr. Gayfeather. I've got to try. He's the sheriff, he may know of some way -—"

Mr. Sabo shook his head. "He has his duty to do, Capri. Once a sheriff, always a sheriff."

"But he wasn't born one," said Capri.

Mr. Sabo smiled pleasantly. "No, of course not. And if there's any way I may help -—may I drive you into the city tomorrow?"

Capri's heart melted. Mr. Sabo was so good. "Thanks," she said, "oh, Mr. Sabo, thanks a million! Nine o'clock?" When Mr.

Sabo agreed, Capri went softly back to the trailer and, without waking Francia, went to bed.

In the sheriff's office the next morning Capri smiled shyly at the secretary and told her she would like to speak to Mr. Gayfeather.

"He's very busy right now," said the young woman. "He's in conference with the Better Government League."

The door opened behind her. Mr. Gayfeather said, "On the contrary, Miss Leeds, I am now in conference with Miss Capri Maccomb. The BGL left by the side door. Come in, Capri. I was wondering when you'd get here."

He was expecting her! Capri's heart sank. It sounded so cynical, as though he guessed that she would be here to beg favors, to plead help.

Mr. Gayfeather waved her to a chair and sat down across from her at his desk. Over his head an Indian maiden canoed determinedly across moonlit waters etched in glowing colors on a calendar.

"And where is your mother?" asked Mr. Gayfeather with interest. "I seem always to be asking her whereabouts, do I not? But has she recovered from the events of last night?"

"No," Capri said. "No, she hasn't. She's still in bed, and when I got up, Mr. Gayfeather, she just turned her face to the wall and refused to talk." She sighed. "That's not like her."

Mr. Gayfeather sighed too, and arose, stuffing his hands into his pockets. "Your mother's ambitious, Capri she's too ambitious."

Capri sat up straight. "And why shouldn't she be? We lost all of our money in the farm. She has me to look after. She wants so much for me, and the carnival was her only hope. All she wanted was to make it the best carnival in the whole country."

Mr. Gayfeather swung around angrily. "Then for pity sake, Capri, why did she risk her first big chance and allow some idiot to set up gambling tables in her carnival?"

Capri stared at him aghast. "You mean you believe that she did?"

Mr. Gayfeather sat down. "I believe what I see. I have to. I'm a sheriff. What would you have me believe?"

Capri could not believe her ears. "I thought --—I hoped you knew us better. I don't know why," she added in a defeated voice.

Mr. Gayfeather leaned back in his chair and studied her, "Capri," he said, "I admire your loyalty. I expect you to be loyal. But there are certain things your mother might not have told you."

Capri jumped to her feet. "So that's what you think! Just like all the others!"

"Capri, sit down. Neither of us must allow our personal feelings to interfere. You must remember that I have a job to do."

"Job!" she cried. "You think we're dishonest, you think we're crooked. I thought you were our friend. I thought you at least would listen when I told you about the fire in Cottsville and how the fire chief said it was set and now this -—"

Mr. Gayfeather looked startled. "What fire?" he asked.

"It was my magic tent. It caught fire. There was a high wind that night, and if it wasn't for Doc and Matt's quick thinking the whole carnival would have burned. It was awful." She said defiantly, "The fireman told me that it was arson. He showed me pieces of a rag used to start the fire."

"I see," said Mr. Gayfeather. "And when did this occur?"

She flushed. "Last Saturday."

Mr. Gayfeather appeared thoughtful. He made a church steeple of his two hands and studied her over them. There was a long, long silence. Capri grew fidgety before it ended. Then at last Mr. Gayfeather frowned. "You wanted me to help, is that it? You thought I might speak to the Better Government League about this?"

Capri nodded hopefully. "You see, we have nowhere to move the carnival." She added apologetically, "and we have no money, either. Not enough to keep us open, that is."

Mr. Gayfeather stood up; he looked regretful. "The Better Government League would not hear me," he said. "What's happened has happened, no one can erase it. Canada City is tired of gamblers and wants to protect itself. They feel cheated now, they feel they have been hoodwinked. Officially, I am afraid there is nothing that can be done for your mother."

Capri turned pale. "There's nothing you can do? Nothing, Mr. Gayfeather?"

He shook his head. "I'm sorry, but my hands are tied. As sheriff of Canada City there's absolutely nothing I could do."

And feeling herself dismissed -—for after all, what else was there to say? -—Capri rose painfully to her feet, and as quietly as possible left the room.

CHAPTER EIGHTEEN

From the sheriff's office Mr. Sabo and Capri drove slowly towards the county jail to meet Doc and arrange for the release of the carny folks.

"Nothing doing?" Mr. Sabo had asked after one quick look at Capri's face.

"Nothing doing," she said. "He was the biggest disappointment of all. I should never, never have asked help from Mr. Gayfeather."

Mr. Sabo smiled. "Very few people are willing to help in time of need."

"I guess you're the only one we can turn to," said Capri soberly.

Doc was awaiting them at the steps of the courthouse, his usually battered hat replaced by a newer one. Mr. Sabo's eyes began to shine, his attitude became one of manager; he was not at all unused to bailing out employees, and it was like old times for him.

"You sure you don't want to wait in the car?" Doc asked as they walked up the steps.

"Me? Of course not," scoffed Capri. "What do you think I am, a baby?"

At the desk Mr. Sabo bowed politely to the Sergeant in charge. "I am from the Toby Brothers Traveling Show," he said, completely ignoring Capri and Doc. "I'm here to retrieve those arrested."

The Sergeant grinned. "You can have 'em. Hey, Red," he shouted, "bring out those carnival people. Bring that Southland chap first, and on a halter. He may bite." In an aside to Mr. Sabo, he said, "doesn't that guy ever sleep? He's been yelling for a lawyer all night."

Mr. Sabo smiled courteously, and they all waited. Presently they were rewarded by the sight of Matt, followed by Captain Southland.

Placidly, with no sign of anger, Captain Southland walked to the desk. "It's true," he inquired of the Sergeant, "that I'm to be released now?"

Mr. Sabo said, "that's right," and peeled off bills from a roll he took from his pocket.

Captain Southland watched the Sergeant count the money, nod and wave his hand. "I'm free now?" asked Captain Southland clearly.

"Right."

Felicity -—Miss Darlene is free also?"

"Yeah," said the sergeant, growing bored.

"Thank you." For the first time Captain Southland faced Capri. His exquisitely pompadoured hair was only slightly ruffled. "Good," he said, and a new tone crept into his voice. "Then you may tell your mother, Miss Maccomb, that never have I been subjected to such indignities. Never. You may inform her, also, please, that I am withdrawing my motordrome from the Toby Brothers Traveling Show and shall be happy never to see it again and will have my head examined, please, if anyone finds me again lowering myself by accepting a position with such a cheap, disreputable, shabby carnival."

Capri fumbled for a bench and sat down. First Mr. Gayfeather, and now this! Something ironical and appropriate that she had learned in school swam to the surface of her mind. You, too, Brutus? she heard herself saying to her private surprise.

"See here," said Doc quickly, "you can't pull out. You've got a contract for the season."

Capri said slowly, "not just a contract, Captain Southland, but my mother paid you a great deal of money to persuade you to come to us."

Captain Southland smiled. "You mentioned a contract, yes?" His left hand brought out a sheet of white paper from his pocket which he happily tore into a dozen pieces. "I had a contract," he announced. "*Had* one. As for the money... He threw several bills on the floor at Capri's feet. "If you want any more of it back you can sue me."

Capri blindly stooped and picked up the money. "Five dollars", she said.

"Exactly." Captain Southland took Felicity's arm. "As I said," he repeated, "your mother may sue me if she dares. Personally, I would like to sue her."

Felicity obediently tossed her head of brilliant black hair, which was not quite so curly or attractive after a night of neglect. At that, she and Captain Southland walked out of the building, and out of Capri and Francia's lives forever.

"What an inspiration he turned out to be," said Doc disgustingly. "The rats always desert a sinking ship."

Matt touched Capri's arm. "Capri," he said in a low voice, "I want to talk to you. It's important."

"Right now?" asked Capri doubtfully.

He nodded. "Let's take the bus back to the field."

"All right, Matt," she said. And, turning to Doc, she asked him to tell Fran that she would be half an hour behind the others. Then they stood on the curbing and watched Mr. Sabo pilot the old truck into traffic. When it had disappeared around the corner Capri drew a deep breath.

"How was it, Matt? Was it awful spending the night in there?"

"It was an experience," he said. "Believe me, it's good to be out. I can almost sympathize with Cap Southland. Only it would take more than that to make me quit the carny," he added warmly.

He took her hand and they walked slowly toward the bus stop. For a few minutes Capri could pretend that nothing was wrong, that they were headed home to the same old carnival, but the feeling could not last.

"Matt," she said, "you may have to quit. They've closed the carny. We have to be moved by six o'clock."

His hands tightened in hers. "You're kidding."

She shook her head. "We have nowhere to go, Matt. And Francia's broke."

His lips tightened. "It sure was a pretty frame up then, wasn't it. Somebody's figuring was just perfect." His voice turned bitter. "Capri, that's what I wanted to tell you. I got to thinking last night when we were in jail. I got to wondering just who did this to you."

She turned an inquiring face to his and waited. "Darn it," he said, "I don't know how to begin."

"Begin what?"

He made a helpless gesture. "Well, I got to thinking. There's one thing i never told you about Jack Last and his pickpocketing."

"What, Matt?" she asked.

He hesitated. Then, "Mr. Sabo put him up to it."

"Mr. Sabo? Oh, Matt, that couldn't be true!"

"It is. I was right there when it was settled. That was the first night you and your mother were here, and Mr. Sabo said he wanted trouble made. Plenty of trouble."

"But why?"

"I don't know. But I got to thinking that it might have been Mr. Sabo who put those wheels in the tent and then called the police."

Capri thought about it a moment, and then shook her head. "I don't think he could have, Matt. Why, he's been wonderful."

Matt frowned. "Then how do you explain his wanting trouble made?"

"Well," replied Capri thoughtfully, "I imagine it was purely out of pique. Didn't you say that was the night we arrived here? Of course, he was angry and hurt, too. He managed the carny for fifteen years, you know. I remember how shocked he was that night to see us. But after he got to know us, why, he grew to like us."

Matt shrugged. "Somebody set that fire, and then framed your mother last night."

Capri smiled. "I know. But honestly, Matt, if you knew how helpful Mr. Sabo has been, giving Fran advice, really good advice, too -—why, he practically ran the whole carny the first few days we were here and saw to it personally that none of the concessionaires cheated Fran out of her percentage."

Matt looked relieved. "Anyway, I've told you," he said, "and it's a load off my mind."

They leaped aboard the bus and settled comfortably in the long rear seat. "If I had a million dollars," said Matt, offering her part of a chocolate bar, "I'd buy the carnival lock, stock and barrel. I do the high dive and you'd be a magician, even better than Houdini or Major Marvel."

"I wish you did have a million dollars, because Mr. Sabo will never offer us that."

"Mr. Sabo?"

She told him about it. "It's practically settled that he's taking over this afternoon."

"Mr. Sabo again," said Matt ominously.

Capri laughed. "Oh, Matt, you might as well accuse Doc or Ma Boone as Mr. Sabo."

"What about that sheriff friend of yours?" he asked.

Capri's smile faded. "Him!" she said scornfully and they lapsed into silence, busy with their own thoughts until they came to the end of the bus line. There, not far away, the roofs of the carnival rose jaggedly over the acres and acres of low grass; Capri and Matt struck out along the road toward it.

"Darn it," said Capri hoarsely, "its a beautiful old carny, isn't it, Matt."

"One of the best," said Matt. "Say, here comes a car. Want to hitch a ride?"

But the long gray car, kicking out dust clouds behind it, came to an abrupt halt beside them. Mr. Gayfeather said, "Hop in, kids."

"What are you doing out here?" asked Capri angrily.

Mr. Gayfeather refused to be baited. He said twinklingly, "Pick her up, Matt, and carry her into the back seat. She looks stubborn as a mule."

"No, thank you, I'll climb in myself," said Capri stiffly. And to Mr. Gayfeather she said despondently, "At least you're in time to see Francia sell the carnival."

"Good gracious," said Mr. Gayfeather, "she mustn't do that."

Capri was startled. "Why?"

Mr. Gayfeather started the car. They soared luxuriously ahead. "Well," he said amiably, "it was quite true that as sheriff of Canada City there was nothing, I could do to help you. And it was quite true that my hands were tied. But if you will glance up here, you'll see my hands are no longer in bondage. Nor am I sheriff of Canada City."

"What?" gasped Capri. "You've stopped being sheriff?"

"It's very simple," explained Mr. Gayfeather. "I discovered that I could not be both a conscientious sheriff and a conscientious friend of the Maccomb family."

"Say," Matt said, grinning," you're all right."

Mr. Gayfeather gave him a reproachful glance. "Don't be misguided," he said humorously. "I am a sensible man. Before taking such a rash course I telephoned first to the Cottsville fire department to confirm Capri's most interesting story."

"And still I might not be here," he added simply, "if I had not thought of a most satisfactory solution to your problem."

CHAPTER NINETEEN

Mr. Sabo and Francia had just settled on a price for the Toby Brothers Traveling Show. It was nowhere near the sum of money he had offered before; it was, in truth, a bargain for Mr. Sabo, but Francia could not be sure of this and anyway the carnival had to be moved out of Canada City by six o'clock or there would be an additional fine. With her mind made-up, Francia wanted only to be rid of the show as quickly as possible; if things move too slowly there was a chance her tears might show themselves, which would embarrass her far more than it would Mr. Sabo. Two weeks ago, she would have been astonished to learn that she would ever grow accustomed to running a carnival, but now the thought of leaving it gave her a curiously empty feeling. It had been a problem at times to her and it was proving a problem now, but it had also proven a joy.

Now she brought out her fountain pen, unscrewed the lid of the ink bottle -—for it would be intolerable, and in very bad taste, too, if the pen should be empty -—and bent over the sheet of paper.

"Here we are, Mr. Gayfeather," said Capri from the door.

Francia put down her pen and turned, unable to conceal her surprise.

"Mr. Gayfeather gave us a ride," explained Capri beaming. "Hello, Mr. Sabo. Mr. Gayfeather has something to say to you, Fran."

"What could he possibly wish to say now?" asked Fran, her voice cool.

"Well," said Capri, "for one thing he is no longer sheriff. He's resigned, Fran."

"Really?"

"Really," said Mr. Gayfeather, removing his hat. "Mrs. Maccomb, after checking on a certain little story of arson in Cottsville, I have wondered if the Canada City authorities we're not only thorough but a trifle rash. You have not yet sold the carnival?"

Francia regarded him with bewilderment. Mr. Sabo said quickly, "we are just about to conclude the sale. If you will excuse us for just a moment?"

"I should like to beg of her not to conclude it," said Mr. Gayfeather.

Mr. Sabo frowned. "I don't believe you realize the circumstances, sir. This carnival must be beyond the city limits by six o'clock. I am helping Mrs. Maccomb out of a tight spot by buying the carnival from her and assuming all the expense of moving it a hundred miles or so."

"That's unnecessary," said Mr. Gayfeather curtly. "I have found a place for this carnival not quite seven miles from here."

"Mr. Gayfeather!" cried Francia. "Where?"

He bowed to her. "Your farm, Mrs. Maccomb. My farm now, but surely you will accept the lending of its fields for the remainder of the week?"

Francia sank back in her chair. Capri let out a whoop. "River Junction!" she cried.

Mr. Sabo smiled. "I am sorry to disappoint you, but you would never be issued a license after this regrettable scandal in Canada City."

Mr. Gayfeather said nothing, but from his pocket extracted a bulky white envelope and tossed it on the table. "I'm sorry to contradict you, Mr. Sabo," he said. "But here is the license. I looked into the matter thoroughly and took the liberty of taking out the license on the spot. My farm lies just over the Canada City line in River Junction. They were very happy to have a carnival visit them."

"Why, this means we can start all over again," cried Francia.

Capri said in sudden panic, "Fran, you want to, don't you?"

"I don't like being thrown out of a city any more than you do," Capri. "Of course, I'm not sorry. I'm glad."

Mr. Sabo's lip curled. "I regret to inform you that you have only the skeleton of a carnival left. Captain Southland has gone, eleven roustabouts quit last night -—I really think you ought to reconsider."

Francia smiled. "It doesn't matter. Nothing matters but getting rid of the reputation we've been given."

Mr. Sabo did not smile. "I need hardly tell you that if anything else should happen I would not care to again make such a generous offer." A muscle twitched in his cheek, and he put up a hand to conceal it.

At the hesitation in Francia's manner," Capria said, "Nothing else will happen, Fran. We won't let it."

Everyone pitched in to help. It was like a party. Slim said he'd never seen a carnival go up so fast. Ma Boone drove tent pegs with the best of them, her long arms flying, while Capri and Matt cut the grass along the midway and burned it in piles. It was almost dark before the midway was cleared out of pastureland, and signs put up, and electricity run down from Mr. Gayfeather's house to the trailers. From the trucks the roustabouts brought the rides, great two-story structures that were reassembled in less than two hours by only a comparative handful of men. It delighted Capri to watch them unfold; it never ceased to fascinate her.

"What time is it now?" asked Francia suddenly.

"It was ten o'clock." She nodded. "We'll open at two tomorrow afternoon and keep going all day."

"How about the magic show?" asked Capri. "Fran, we'll need everything possible to close up the gaps in the midway. Couldn't we somehow try Archie in the Bingo tent?"

Doc smiled. "I'll tell you what. Slim and me could easily knock together a stage in the morning. How about it, Mrs. Maccomb?"

She returned his smile warmly. "Call me Francia, Doc," she said. "We've no need for formality. We're all carny folks."

Capri could hardly believe her ears and almost said so.

"There goes the Ferris wheel up," said Matt. And they cheered it, for that was the trademark of the carnival, the oldest, the showiest, and still the best.

This is a far cry from Canada City, thought Capri. We're smaller than ever before and shabbier than ever, but we're still all together. Aloud she said, "Ready to go back to the trailer, Fran?"

"Yes," she said. But for a few minutes Francia lingered, her gaze on the Ferris wheel. At last she said, "It's nice. Wonderfully nice." She reached over and took Capri's hand. Capri was surprised to see tears in her eyes. Francia said softly. "Why did he do it? It wasn't necessary. Not to him."

"I think," said Capri slowly, "because he didn't like to see us get hurt."

Francia's clasp tightened, and then she suddenly released her hand. "Capri."

"Yes?"

"Am I still attractive?"

"In the darkness Capri smiled. "Yes, Fran, you are. You're lovely, and I guess you'll always be."

In the morning Capri awoke to the sound of hammering and subdued shouting—cheerful, busy sounds. With the little laugh she ran to the door and flung it wide, drawing in deep draughts of clear country air. The sun had been up for hours, there was smoke coming from the cookhouse chimney, and down the dirt road from the barn model three fat red hens, shaking their heads as they came like disapproving old ladies.

Dew still lingered in the deep grass. It was going to be a hot day, with a mist slow to burn off. Real June carny weather and, depleted as the show was, there was a sure promise in the air of a good evening.

Capri dressed quickly and went down to the midway. Francia and Doc had gone out to post advertisements of the carnival in conspicuous places, Matt was driving the last nail into the improvised stage, and Archie was unpacking his magician's paraphernalia.

The professor lightly stroked the white suit and the gold cummerbund. "It'll be nice wearing it again," he said shyly. "Molly's polishing up the spangles on her tights."

It would be hard to overlook the corner where Captain Southland's motordrome should stand. If only he could have been persuaded to remain a few days longer, thought Capri, what a difference it would make in the look and feel of the carny.

Ma Boone was scrubbing her sign clean. "Morning, Capri," she said. "At least we can't complain about the weather. Happy June to you, dearie. It's your birthday month, isn't it?"

"That's right."

"We'll have to give you a party." She directed a hard look about her and sighed. "I sure hate to see it a two-bit carny now. This show's like a child to me."

Capri smiled. "Once I'd have jumped on you for saying it's two-bit now, but I guess you love it more than any of us."

"Well," said Ma tartly, "til somebody promises me that Heaven's got a nice carnival, this is where you'll find me."

Capri kicked doggedly at a rock. "I wish there was something we could do right now. Don't we look small? Like a garden party or a -—a Girl Scout encampment."

"Listen," said Ma, putting her hands on her hips and giving Capri a stern glance, "you need a real good feature act, something to get people to this part of the town and keep 'em here."

"Of course, we need that," mourned Capri.

Ma deliberately looked away to where Matt had paused in his hammering to watch them. "Capri," she said, "you've got all the makings of a record-breaker right here in this carny. And what's more there's somebody who could put this show on the map and keep it there."

"Are you serious, Ma? Who?"

"Matt Lincoln."

Capri let out a peal of laughter. "Oh, Ma" she started to say, and then with a start noticed the lack of humor in those heavily lashed black eyes. The laughter died abruptly on Capri's lips. "You're not serious. I won't listen to you."

"Why?" asked Ma calmly. "Because he's a friend of yours? Does that make him something special?"

Capri jumped to her feet. "No," she cried. "No, of course not. But -—why, that's dangerous. Much too dangerous!"

Ma gave a brief smile. "He wants to do it, doesn't he? Why, he's over there right now hangin' on our every expression. He talked to me about it just a few minutes ago. Yes, he wants to do it, Capri. And the carny needs him."

"He put you up to this!"

"No," said Ma, "he talked to me about it, to me and Doc. We both thought it a fine idea. Not to dive one hundred and ten feet -—not at first -—but to start his diving, nevertheless."

"He hasn't practiced!"

Ma sighed. "There is no real practicin', Capri. There's only the doin' of it."

"That's exactly what I mean," cried Capri.

"If he weren't Matt Lincoln -—if you heard about his performin' at a bigger carny, you'd feel differently."

Capri put her hands to her ears. "I won't listen. I won't hear of such a thing!"

"Your mother may."

Capri burst into tears. She had never been so furious. "I think you're dreadful suggesting such a thing. Yes, you and Matt and Doc, all of you. Why, he might be killed!"

"Well, now," said Ma, "that's a risk Captain Southland took, now didn't he?"

Capri and Ma stared at each other for a long, silent moment. But ma did not say, "there, there, Capri, I know how you feel, no carnies worth your tears." Her face did not soften at all.

Capri drew a long breath. "If the carny's worth that much to you, then you can have it!"

She walked violently away, but at the end of the midway she turned as though she might not have made her point clear after all. "He can't do it," she cried, but the wind flung it back in her face. He can't, he can't, he can't, she cried silently, and turned her back on them all.

At lunch Francia was preoccupied. She ate with a handful of lists at her plate and studied them busily between bites and sips. Capri stared at her moodily and said nothing. If Ma could feel as she did, then it was quite possible Francia would feel the same way, for in one sense Ma was hideously right -—one-hundred-and-ten-foot jump would indeed put their carnival on the map. But, oh, not Matt. Not Matt.

"What in the world's the matter with you this noon?" asked Fran, looking up. "You seem to be talking to yourself, and not too happy about what you're saying, either. I should think you'd be excited, today of all days."

She wasn't. Not now. The very humbleness of the carnival was a threat. No one had thought such dangerous thoughts while Captain Southland was around.

"Fran," she begged, "if Ma should talk to you please don't listen to her."

Fran's eyebrows shot up. "But I always listen to Ma Boone. She's an extremely wise and shrewd old lady, darling."

"Well," said Capri helplessly, "if you could just promise not to take any of her advice without telling me first. Please, Fran?"

Francia shrugged. "Of course, I wouldn't. This is your carnival, too."

Well, that was something, thought Capri, and with a lighter heart cheerfully scraped the dishes and stacked them in the sink.

CHAPTER TWENTY

The afternoon show brought out a decent crowd, but nothing like their other days, and the crowd was made up mostly of children who were, of necessity, forced to ration their number of rides. As Doc said, they were good advertisers. They might very well go home and bully their parents into returning that night. "But the trouble with just children," he said, scowling, "is they spend their money on the rides and not on the concessions. If things get tough the concessionaires will just move on. We can't afford to lose them, either. There are few enough of them."

Even Professor Archibald, the Wizard of Wizardry, performed for a humiliatingly small audience. He remained the perfect showman, but it was a strain on him to pretend that the applause was overwhelming.

Capri left the midway and wandered up the hill in the direction of the springhouse. It was cool there, and she wanted to think, but from the front porch of the farmhouse, Mr. Gayfeather hailed her. He was leaning back on two legs of a chair, his pipe in his mouth, and his feet on the rail.

"Come up and sit with me," he said. "Admire the view. It isn't every farmer has a view like this."

Capri sprawled out on the top step fanned herself. "It's hot," she said.

Mr. Gayfeather stood up. "Do come in and see the house," he begged. "It's newly papered and delightfully cool."

Capri obediently rose to her feet and followed him.

There was a striped pattern of wallpaper in the hall.

"That's very nice," she said.

There was a flowered design in the dining room.

"That's very nice," she said.

Mr. Gayfeather went into the kitchen and returned with two glasses of iced root beer.

"Thank you," said Capri, "this is very nice."

Mr. Gayfeather placed his hands on his hips and stared down at her sternly. "Has your vocabulary grown smaller? Or aren't you paying me any attention?" he said. "You have three times said the word nice. Is there something wrong?"

"N-no," Capri answered, and promptly burst into tears again.

Mr. Gayfeather handed her a handkerchief and thoughtfully guided her into the study. "Sit down," he said. "Tell me about it."

Capri sniffed. "All I seem to do is cry. I haven't -—I don't know what to do. Something terrible has happened."

"Why, my dear," said Mr. Gayfeather, startled. "What in the world can it be?"

She said slowly, "Matt wants to take Captain Southland's place as the main attraction. And Doc and Ma Boone -—they agree!"

"I had no idea that Matt rode a motorcycle," said Mr. Gayfeather.

Capri shook her head. "You don't understand. He wants to dive from a one-hundred-and-ten-foot platform into a tank of water. A very small tank of water."

"Good gracious!" cried Mr. Gayfeather.

She nodded. "Apparently, it's an -—an obsession with him. He's an acrobat. He thinks it's the only way to get started. He wants to do it."

"Has it been done?" asked Mr. Gayfeather curiously. "*Can* it be done?"

"I don't know," she said miserably. "I don't know."

"And you say Ma and Doc are sympathetic?"

She bit her lip angrily. "Yes. They think it all right for him to begin at one hundred feet, anyway."

Mr. Gayfeather stood up and began pacing the floor. "He's a young fool," he said. "An out and out fool, of course. You didn't say yes?"

"Me? Oh, no, Mr. Gayfeather." She shivered. "I couldn't. Not ever."

"It's the most ridiculous thing I've ever heard of," went on Mr. Gayfeather. "Sheer suicide. What does he want to do it for?"

"I suppose -—I suppose he thinks we need something like that rather badly. And nobody else would take him on, he's so

168

young. And it takes money to get started. But I never thought -—I just never took him seriously."

"And so the young fool puts himself in your hands, is that it? You've not mentioned it yet to your mother?"

Capri shook her head.

"Well, tell her about it," said Mr. Gayfeather. "It's up to her, anyway." He swung around and shook a finger at her. "All you have to do, mark my words, is tell her. No woman would dream of allowing an eighteen-year-old boy -—or anybody -—do such a ridiculous thing. She'd never take the responsibility. Stop worrying about it at once, my dear. Just tell your mother. She's a woman."

Capri drew a deep sigh of relief. Thinking about it carefully she nodded her head. Yes, she might count on Francia. Her mother had never wished for anything more than her happiness. Capri smiled. "I'll do that," she said. "I'll tell Francia. And thank you, Mr. Gayfeather."

"You mustn't go until you finish your root beer," he said. "Now tell me, do you like the study?"

Following his glance, Capri saw that he was staring at the portrait of Fran and Uncle Shoe that reached clear to the ceiling. It was like coming home to see that, thought Capri. The furniture in the room was strange but not unfriendly, not with the picture of her mother and her uncle suspended from the wall like ghosts of another day.

Mr. Gayfeather smiled. "You're looking at my favorite picture," he said. "Many a night I've sat there in that same chair you're in, studying her, wondering about her."

"Her?"

"Francia Abbott Maccomb. Your mother, my dear. Who else? Your uncle I would have enjoyed knowing, but your mother I have enjoyed looking at."

Capri allowed her gaze to return to the picture. "I like it too," she acknowledged. "She looks so gracious. As though nothing ever really touched her."

Mr. Gayfeather seemed startled, and then he grinned boyishly. "Come here, Capri," he said, and as she obeyed his face turned gay. "I want to tell you something. Sit there on that stool. It will make it easier for me. I want to tell you -—"

"What?" asked Capri, as he hesitated.

Mr. Gayfeather took a deep breath. "I want you to know that I've fallen very deeply in love with your mother."

Capri was so surprised that she almost fell off the stool. "You?" she gasped. "But you -—you've been so—- "

"Quite so. We've appeared to dislike one another, you mean." He was smiling. "I think you ought to know that I fell in love first of all with her portrait." He sighed. "That sounds very strange and young of me. But I have been lonely. When I was a young man, I worked desperately hard because I had so little. I became astonishingly successful. So successful that I was able to retire early from my little manufacturing business."

He gave her a slight smile, as though apologizing for taking up her time with such a small thing as his life. "When at last I retired to live in Canada City, I found that I had worked so hard all my life that I had neglected to make friends, to form a way of life. That is very important, you know."

"Why, that's like Francia and Uncle Shoe," cried Capri. "Really it is. They worked dreadfully hard, they made lots of money, but when they came here -—" she halted lamely, not wanting to sound critical, but wondering at the same time how such a thing could happen to so many people.

"That is something that luckily you will never experience," said Mr. gayfeather, smiling. "I'm delighted, because I'm fond of you."

"But what did you do? Where did you go?" asked Capri, deeply interested.

He grinned. "I went into politics. I became sheriff. Oh, not immediately, but it happened. That was when I decided to find myself a real home. So I bought your farm."

He hesitated. "I don't know how to make you understand about this, my dear. At first your mother's portrait was simply a lovely thing to me, the very epitome of what I had dreamed of all my life. But then it came to me, gradually, That your mother was a real person, not simply a painted creature on campus. I wondered what had happened to you. I made inquiries of Mr. Callandar, but he was extremely evasive. I thought I might never see you again."

"And then we turned up," laughed Capri.

"Yes," said Mr. Gayfeather, "you turned up."

"And you didn't even recognize Francia."

Mr. Gayfeather smiled. "That's life, Capri. That is cold reality. In all the storybooks your mother would have appeared to me just as young and exquisite as in the portrait on that wall. But, at the time we met, I thought only what a disagreeable woman this is shouting at me and waving her arms."

Capri nodded. "She was cross and excited that day."

Mr. Gayfeather smiled. "Of course, she was; human beings often are. I was disappointed," went on Mr. Gayfeather, "and yet at the same time I was curiously relieved. I am afraid I could never have lived up to the Francia on the wall. But this Francia was real. She was tired and confused and, to me, far lovelier than that lifeless picture. She made me feel young again, and alive."

Mr. Gayfeather turned and looked at the portrait. "I find I want more than anything else in the world to make your mother happy. To take care of her. To restore her serenity." He glanced at Capri and frowned. "She ought never to have left the farm. I believe she loved it more than you do. You're young," he said quietly, "and I have an idea, Capri, that you are a great deal like your Uncle Shoe. I think you could be happy anywhere, among any people."

"Oh, but I love the farm, too," said Capri.

Mr. Gayfeather stood up, his hands in his pockets. "Yes, you do," he said, "but you also love the carnival. That is why your mother has been frightened for you and wants so much for you."

"I know." Capri sighed and stood up. "What are you going to do now, Mr. Gayfeather?"

He grinned. "I'm going to ask her to marry me. Will you mind very much?"

Her face lighted up. "Mind? Oh, my goodness, no. I think it would be terrific. When?"

"When I think she'll say yes. Now run along. And not a word from you, promise?"

"Promise!"

She could hardly contain her joy. He was exactly right for Francia, and when Francia realized this, as someday she surely must, she would have the farm again, with all the time in the world to enjoy it and be the gracious lady once more. And never again will she have to wrestle alone with shabbiness and old bills and a carnival.

Capri gave a childish hop-skip-and-a-jump and hurried towards their trailer. Francia would now settle once and for all any idea of Matt's launching his suicidal career with the Toby Brothers Traveling Show.

CHAPTER TWENTY-ONE

From the trailers up and down the hill there came the rich aroma of frying bacon, pot roast, and steak. From their own trailer there was only silence, and not a sign of activity. Capri anxiously pushed open the door.

Francia was quietly knitting, the radio tuned softly to a musical program. She glanced up as Capri entered and gave her a slight, absent smile. "There's tuna fish salad in the refrigerator," she said, "and Ma Boone brought over a slice of watermelon."

"Aren't you eating?"

"I already have, darling. I'd about given you up."

"I was talking to Mr. Gayfeather and seeing the house."

"Oh," Francia said, dropping a stitch, "Matt was here."

"What did he want?" Capri asked angrily.

Francia shrugged. "He said he'd talked to you later."

Capri sat down across from her and swung her legs. "Fran," she said carefully, "are you happy now?"

"Happy?" Francia smiled. "Well, I'm not too happy about what's been happening. But if you mean the carnival, darling. I don't mind it as I did at first." She sighed. "But it still belongs more to you than to me. You've done a good job, Capri, especially with the magic show. You and Mr. Sabo have both done so much more than I."

Capri was scarcely listening. She watched Fran's nimble fingers pushing at the gay wool and automatically followed her gestures. "You dropped one there, Fran."

"Darn it," Fran said good humoredly.

It was like old times at the farm; they were close again. When the dropped stitch had been collected. Capri began to pour out her story.

"It's Matt, Fran. And Doc and Ma agree with him. And Mr. Gayfeather says --—"

"What in the world are you talking about?" asked Francia.

"Matt. He wants an act of his own."

"What does he do? "asked Francia.

"He wants," said Capri bitterly, "to break his fool neck." As she explained to Francia, she was silently begging her to understand. "It's so dangerous, Fran. He's only eighteen. I know he's a wonderful acrobat, but he doesn't have to do things like this. He wants to get into vaudeville. He thinks there are still opportunities there."

"You say he's been practicing. Where and how?"

"At the lake in Cottsville. Only, of course, there's no real practicing for a stunt like that, just -—just the doing of it."

Francia nodded. "He's quite right, of course. It's time he was getting started. One doesn't do acrobatic tricks at fifty."

"Oh, yes, I know, but -—"

"You want me to forbid Matt's diving in our carnival, is that it? You feel it's too risky?"

"Yes," said Capri." You will, won't you?"

Francia laid down the knitting and crossed her hands in her lap. She closed her eyes. "Let me see if I understand this. Matt believes that he can dive from a hundred-foot platform into a tank of water. He wants to do it, and Doc and Ma think it worthwhile. You disagree. You believe it's dangerous."

"That's right," said Capri eagerly.

"Of course, it's dangerous," nodded Francia, opening her eyes.

"But if you forbid it -—" cried Capri. "You're going to, aren't you?"

Francia said in a low voice, "No. No, I'm not going to, Capri."

"Fran!"

"I said I'm not going to. I couldn't."

Capri caught her breath. She had turned scarlet with astonishment and fear. She said slowly, "you're thinking of the money it would bring in. Oh, Francia, you're thinking of the publicity, of getting ahead, of making more money. How could you, how could you?"

Francia shook her head. "That's not true, Capri. I'm just the usual human being who makes a great many mistakes but learns, I hope, from each of them."

"Mistakes!" shouted Capri, frantic. "I don't think you are a human being! How can you let Matt do a thing like that! You said -—"

"Capri!"

She stopped and looked in wonder at Francia. Francia had not moved, nor had she raised her voice above a whisper. She was steady, sure.

"There's no need to say things you'll regret later, Capri. I'm thinking of you as much as I'm thinking of Matt. If he wants to do that stunt, nobody on earth is going to stop him. You can delay him. But you can't stop him, Capri."

"Well, we could certainly discourage him," Capri cried. "He could wait."

Francia said, quietly, "you're afraid, Capri, aren't you. You're afraid something might happen to him. You're hiding your head in the sands, aren't you. You're like I am, but you don't know vaudeville, do you. You don't know show business. I hope you never would. What insane notion made me choose the carnival, I shall never guess. Sheer desperation, of course. I should have realized at once that with the blood of two theatricals in you -—"

"Two?" repeated Capri. "You mean one. Father wasn't -—"

Francia shook her head. "Father was."

"What on earth do you mean?" faltered Capri.

Francia sighed. "Your father was not really a banker, Capri."

"What?" she gasped.

"No, Francia wheeled upon her. "Oh, yes, he worked in a bank for six months before you were born. He worked there very patiently because, you see, I did not want him on the stage. But when you were born, he quietly left me."

"Mother!"

"Yes, he left me. He went back to vaudeville."

Capri's mouth opened in surprise. Francia refused to look at her. He was Major Marvel, the magician."

Capri took a long, long breath. "But I've heard of him," she whispered.

"So you see," went on Francia gently, "he was never really a banker. I wanted him to be. I tried to make him one. But instead, I only made him very unhappy. He couldn't live without the stage."

"Then he wasn't killed in a train accident?"

Francia stood very still. "That part is true. I never had a chance to tell him how sorry I was."

"Oh, Mother."

Francia sat down suddenly as though her knees could no longer support her. "So now you know my secret," she said. "I shall never quite forgive this carnival for bringing it out and making it known to you." A sad little smile crossed her lips. "But I cannot allow you to make the same mistake of trying to fashion someone else's life to fit your own."

They were silent. Francia added softly, "No, really, Capri, you must face up to it. I'm sorry it's happened, but, you see, I could not take Matt's chances away from him. If this is his world, if this is what he wants, if what he proposes to do is dangerous, then that's too bad -—but it's show business. It's the carnival world, it's the circus world, it's the vaudeville world. But if he's not made for it -—if it's too much for him, as it was for me -—then he'll come down from that platform, and I'm sure that I for one will be very happy to see him fail."

"You mean -—*you* mean he could get up there and change his mind."

"Of course. He may very well change it in a hurry. But I shan't refuse him, and neither will you. If you do then you'll be afraid of other things, too, for the rest of your life. As I have been. But no one must destroy his purpose." Her hands clenched into a tight fist. "Believe me, Capri, for I know."

Capri looked up at her mother, and suddenly reached out to touch her cheek. She saw Francia as an individual, a person who had made mistakes and suffered for them and gone on to try to build a new life.

And that's how it will be for me, too, she thought wonderingly. Only Francia wants my mistakes to be smaller, and not so important as hers were.

And then Francia said a strange thing. She spoke as though to a third person in the room to whom she must explain herself.

"All I wanted," she said, "was a garden. A little garden where I could raise roses and lobelia and delphiniums -—and live richly and quietly."

And that was the tragedy, thought Capri. Francia had known applause and honor and royalty, when all she had ever wanted was to live simply and unobtrusively.

CHAPTER TWENTY-TWO

Capri had gone to bed early, intent on avoiding both Matt and Francia. She had not slept well, her dreams had swung from fantasies of Major Marvel to frightening acrobatics, so that now, opening her eyes suddenly to the darkness she could not be sure whether she had been awakened by a nightmare or by a noise.

All was quiet. The luminous clock on the night table told her that it was three o'clock in the morning. Just three. There was a popular song about that. She turned over on her side and tried to remember the tune of it.

Across the narrow aisle Francia slept tranquilly in the twin bunk. Without a quiver of conscience, thought Capri angrily, without any regard to what she had set in motion.

What if Matt should go through with it? Capri thought, tensing under the sheet. By closing her eyes, she, too, stood at the top of the scaffolding that Fran had ordered built. She, too, stared down at a blur of gaping faces until in her mind she stood upon a platform as high as the Empire State Building. Capri shook her head, trying to clear it. She was turning dizzy merely from the thought of it.

"We have the lumber," Francia had told Doc. "If Matt goes through with it, if he's a success, we'll see about a professional affair built of steel. Could you knock it together for tomorrow night?"

And Doc had said, "Oh, yes, Francia, easily."

To Matt, Francia had said, "you understand it's only a tryout. If you change your mind -—whether in ten minutes, an hour, or not until tomorrow night when you're up there with this spotlight on you -—it's all right with me. You understand that, Matt?"

But Matt had looked at Francia as though she were Santa Claus and had just given him the world. It had been depressing, Capri decided.

She and Matt were enemies now. They had to be, for Capri knew that if she saw Matt alone for even one minute, her control would vanish, and she would turn into a foolish stranger.

Lying there in bed Capri clenched her teeth savagely. Only Matt knew how frightened she was, but she would not spoil it for him by letting it show; if this was what he wanted then, as Francia had said, she could not burden him with her fears. But no one could prevent her from lying in bed at night and dreading it, wanting to hide somewhere until it was over. Of them all, only Mr. Sabo had been on her side. For a moment, upon hearing of it, he had looked almost wild. It was comforting to remember that someone shared her feelings.

"If you continue in such foolishness," he had told Francia, "I shall have to leave this carnival."

"But why?" Francia had demanded.

"Never mind why." He had clamped his mouth shut. It was the first time they had ever seen him upset.

From outside there suddenly came to Capri's ears the sounds of steps moving through the tall grass, pausing, going on, stopping, moving on. A dog, mused Capri, and then frowned, realizing that whatever it was must have been motionless out there for a long time. The movement produced a queer rustling whose very furtiveness brought an eerie sensation to Capri's heart.

Very quietly Capri bent her head below the window shade and peered through into the darkness. She saw nothing at first. Then, as her eyes accustomed themselves to the night, she could make out the shapes of the trailers against the blacker shapes of the carnival tents; and at last, moving between the two, she saw the dim blur of a man.

Well, that's surprising, she thought.

He was stealing soundlessly across the grass, bent low in an effort to make himself small. His back was to Capri. He was crawling away from their trailer, and she guessed that he had taken momentary refuge beneath her window. It had been this that awakened her.

Then two things happened at once. A baby began to cry, a light flew on in the Nebbs' trailer, and the man, startled, ducked low and disappeared --—but not before Capri had seen that it was Mr. Sabo.

That's funny, she thought, and frowned. But what was stranger was that he had been acting almost as though he were hiding.

She creased her forehead in deep thought. It was really nothing. Perhaps he couldn't sleep. Then surely, he had the right, he above all people, to walk softly down to the carnival and look things over.

"But he wasn't just walking softly," she whispered, trying to find the exact adjective. "He was *stealing* down."

She came to an abrupt decision. "I can't sleep, either. I'll just follow and see what's the matter."

Hastily she found her dungarees and pulled them on over her pajamas, reached for a heavy sweater, and carefully opened and closed the door.

It smelled like dawn. Capri took a deep breath, and then walked quietly down the path to the carnival.

Mr. Sabo was nowhere to be seen. Instinctively, without realizing that she was being clever, she paused beside Madame Zela's tent and waited.

She waited a long time. There was not a sound other than a faint wind tangling the fruit trees to the north. Capri grew impatient. Then suddenly, like a star, a light appeared at the very top of the Ferris wheel. It moved and, with a little sigh, she realized Mr. Sabo had climbed the Ferris wheel and had shown a flashlight.

Repairs? But there was plenty of time for that in the morning. If not repairs, what then?

Slowly Capri moved forward until she stood at the base of the Ferris wheel. "Mr. Sabo," she said in a loud, clear voice, "what are you doing up there?"

For a moment there was only silence. Then Mr. Sabo said softly, "Who's there?"

"It's Capri. What are you doing?"

Again, came the voice, even softer now. "Are you alone?"

"Yes, of course."

Something heavy crashed at capri's feet. She bent to pick it up. It was a heavy wrench.

Capri clapped her hand to her mouth. It could not have fallen. It had been thrown. That was when she *knew*.

She was terrified, not for herself but for all of them, for the innocence with which they had dealt with him, for the way they had misconstrued his smiles, his kindnesses. One by one these moments rolled over Capri as she stood there with the wrench in her hand, and they almost suffocated her with their thoroughness. Now, now at last, she recalled the anger with which he had received the news of their moving to the farm; now she could remember the odd way he had acted at the fire in Cottsville when the damage had been less than expected.

She did not pause to reason why. She only knew that she was right -—that by this one act of malevolence Mr. Sabo had supplied her with the missing piece of the puzzle. With this one clue the rest could easily be filled in.

"Capri? Capri?" came the whisper from above. "Did I hurt you? You startled me. I've dropped my tool."

She stepped deeper into the shadows, her heart beating faster. For if the wrench had fallen it would have dropped in a straight line to the ground beneath the wheel; it would have struck the arms of the wheel, clattering and banging on its way down. Instead, it had been hurled with great force at the sound of her voice. She must be careful.

Now the beam of his flashlight was playing over the ground, searching for her. Mr. Sabo said uncertainly, "Capri?"

"I'm right here," she said coldly. "I asked what you were doing up there."

A breathless laugh floated down to her. "Why, I noticed a loose bolt yesterday, my dear. It worried me."

"Won't it keep until morning? And why didn't you turn the Ferris wheel around so that you could work on it down here?"

Mr. Sabo appeared to be thinking that one over, but his flashlight did not rest for an instant. It was a strong light, and it pierced the darkness as a sharp knife cuts cheese. He would have to find her to fight her.

Softly, Capri said, "Will anyone believe you when I tell them you're making repairs at half-past three in the morning?"

"I'll come down. Don't go," said Mr. Sabo. Then "Ha!" he cried, and Capri's breath caught in her throat. His light had found her shoes. That slender sheath of brightness began to move upward towards her face. She recoiled, stepping backwards. She pressed against knobs, something hard, a lever, and as Mr. Sabo's flashlight whistled through the air beside her, the Ferris wheel began to turn. Accidentally, she had set it in motion.

Down, down came Mr. Sabo. She could see him now, see the shape of him crouched on a crossbeam against the blue-black sky. In another moment he would leap off the Ferris wheel. She fought with the controls, pushing everything in a blind effort to stop him.

The Ferris wheel paused and then, with the giddy speed, moved backward. Mr. Sabo reached out, almost fell, and then regained his balance. Capri shouted, Doc! Matt! Fran! Slim! Charlie! Help!

"Capri," shouted Mr. Sabo, "you're acting like a child. Let me down. I'll explain." Slowly, arduously, he began to climb down. She found another lever and shoved it. Again the Ferris wheel spun crazily.

Matt! Doc! Fran!

Strangely enough it was Mr. Gayfeather's light at the farmhouse that went on first. Then a light appeared in Doc's trailer. She heard someone running and then, so suddenly that it blinded her, all the lights along the midway leaped at her.

Doc said, "For gracious sakes, Capri, what's going on here?"

When she spoke, her voice was hysterical. "It's him! Mr. Sabo!"

Beside her, Mr. Gayfeather said, "It's alright, Capri. What's the matter!"

"He's up there. Ask him what he's doing. He almost hit me with his wrench. Doc, he's the one! Don't you see?"

"Now, now," said Doc. "Hey, Nick, what are you up to?"

"My dear Boone," said Mr. Sabo, "what do you think I'm doing? I admit it's an odd hour for repairs, but I couldn't sleep. The child's practically accusing me of all sorts of crimes."

Doc laughed. "Listen, Capri," he said, "what's the matter? Did you have a nightmare or something? Hey, Nick, come down and go to bed."

But Mr. Gayfeather put out a restraining hand. "Just a moment," he said, "you're forgetting some things, Doc. You're making too little of this. Capris no fool."

"What do you mean?" asked Doc.

"Mr. Sabo," said Mr. Gayfeather, "why did you set the fire at Cottsville? For what purpose did you frame Mrs. Maccomb in Canada City?"

There was only the sound of the wind rising and falling, singing between the girders of the giant wheel. Capri raised her glance, shielding her eyes against the light with her hand. The figure at the top of the Ferris wheel was motionless and silent. It was eerie, sinister, the way Mr. Sabo clung there, not even glancing down, frozen like a round, shapeless cocoon to a flower.

With a startled question on her lips Francia joined them. But there was no need for her to speak. One glance at their faces and she, too, glance skyward.

With a muttered cry Doc went to the controls and began turning the Ferris wheel. Mr. Sabo tried to resist by climbing higher, but there was no escape against the relentless pool of the wheel. In a moment he had been brought to earth like a fallen bird. Mr. Gayfeather reached for his arm.

"This is utter nonsense," said Mr. Sabo through stiff, pale lips. "Let me go!"

"Perhaps," said Mr. Gayfeather, "perhaps you would like to explain what repairs you were making."

Mr. Sabo wet his lips carefully. "I don't understand all this fuss. I'm -—" He said angrily, "You can't prove a thing!"

Mr. Gayfeather turned to Francia. "It's true," he said, "we can't prove a thing. Not unless one of us goes for a ride on the Ferris wheel to see just what repairs he was making."

Francia turned pale. Please don't take any chances.

Mr. Gayfeather smiled. "On the contrary. Supposing we ask Mr. Sabo to take a ride on the Ferris wheel." Mr. Sabo's mouth sagged. He looked terrified. "No," he shouted, "no, don't! Please -—please, don't you understand? I won't do it!"

"Why, what do you mean?" asked Mr. Gayfeather. "You were repairing it, weren't you?"

"Yes. No. That is -—"thread by thread, Mr. Sabo was unwinding, like a coat coming apart at the seams. He mopped his forehead. "No, don't make me get on it! No! It's fixed so that it'll breakdown when it gets to the top with anyone in it."

Francia's eyes were blazing. "And I called you a friend!" she whispered.

"Well, for gracious sakes," said Doc. "Nick Sabo, of all people!"

"And you started the fire in Cottsville? And planted the wheels in the tent?"

Mr. Sabo covered his face with his hands. "Yes, yes," he cried. "Yes. Please -—"

"Why?"

Mr. Sabo pointed at Francia, "She had no right -—it was mine, mine, the carnival. I was running it all right. Why, I made more money in a week than she'll ever see in a month."

"Take him, Doc," said Mr. Gayfeather sternly, "I'll get my car. We'll pay the Canada City police an unexpected visit."

"Oh, "Capri, whispered Fran, "what fools we've been."

A harsh, familiar voice bellowed at them down the midway. "What in tarnation's goin' on here? I declare, can't an old woman get some sleep?"

Ma Boone strode among them, clad in a long, billowing white nightgown, a tent stake held in her hand like a gun. Behind her, out of breath, ran Matt."

Capri grinned. "You'll catch your death of cold, Ma."

"I'd have been here sooner, but I dropped my teeth," said Ma. "Matt's a good boy. He stopped to find 'em. Now for what reason have I been waked out of a sound sleep?"

"It's not important, " smiled Capri. "We caught Mr. Sabo sabotaging the Ferris wheel, and now he's going to jail."

Ma looked Mr. Sabo over with cold, level eyes. "Is that all?" she said. "Well, seems to me you could have made a quieter thing of it." And, turning her back on him, she walked straight back to her trailer, her long black pigtails dancing indignantly down her back.

CHAPTER TWENTY-THREE

They were old hands at it now. The gates had opened its six. Charlie Marconi had just the proper amount of dimes and pennies for change and, if any pickpockets had gone to the trouble to come, they had declared a holiday and brought their wives along. As if to make up for all the disagreeable incidences of the past, everything was going off without a hitch.

In fact, people who were cool towards carnivals and towards the Toby Brothers Traveling Show in particular, were among the first to arrive. The Ferris wheel was especially in demand because Canada City, determined to give credit where credit was due, had retracted all of its charges on the front page of the late afternoon newspaper. The Better Government League had issued a public apology and an invitation to the carnival to return later in the season. And for those who read this with great interest, there were assured further thrills at the show by the one-hundred-foot dive of a young man named Matt Lincoln who would perform at midnight.

It was not midnight yet, but it already seemed to Capri as though there were clocks everywhere, as though their hands could not or would not stand still. She had her job to do. She was the only person available to help Archie saw Molly in two in the magic tent. She was Molly's feet, and each time she was wheeled off the platform and escaped from the tiny door it seemed as though the clocks had leaped forward another hour.

"You're not getting all my signals," said Archie at last, gently but reproachfully.

"Oh, Archie, I'm sorry," she said, flushing. "I certainly didn't mean to ruin anything."

"It was nothing," said Archie, "not really. Perhaps if you pay a little closer attention?"

"Yes, of course," Capri said.

But during the next act Archie had to rap three times on the platform before she heard. Capri was mortified as she climbed out.

"Archie," she began.

"Never mind," said Francia, appearing from nowhere. "Shove off, darling, I'll take your place."

"You?" said Capri. "Oh, Fran, did Archie send for you? Did he?"

"Of course not," lied Francia gallantly. "I just thought you might like to have the next hour off. It's the last. Run and see Matt if you'd like."

But Capri did not want to see Matt. Not just yet -—not with a whole hour or more to be afraid for him. She could not bear to see him yet. She walked out of the tent and leaned weakly against the ropes, her cheeks hot.

"Hello," said Slim, smiling down at her. "Tired?"

"Oh, no. Not at all." She shook her head. "By the way, what time is it now?"

"Twenty-five past eleven." He leaned carefully against the canvas and watched the crowds drift by them. "This is like old times," he said. "Looks like your mother can write her own ticket from now on with the sky the limit. But I can't help thinking of Nick Sabo, Capri."

She sighed. "I know, Slim."

Slim shook his head. "We used to think nobody came smarter than Nick Sabo. But I guess in the end he got too smart for his own good."

"Mr. Gayfeather says he wasn't quite sane, maybe at first but not after a while."

Slim nodded. "It figures. There wasn't any sense to the way he kept tryin' and tryin' to run your mother out of business. No sense at all. Just an obsession." Slim sighed. "I guess we all want to possess the things we love. It was just in his blood."

They stood silently for awhile, and then Slim said, easing out his words carefully, "but I guess Nick Sabo's not the first on your mind tonight. I guess you're worried. I'm sorry, Capri."

She said bitterly, "I'm not going to burst into tears and make a fool of myself, if that's what you mean. It's just -—something could go wrong so easily, Slim."

"Now, now Capri."

"Well, it's true enough. You know that."

Slim said slowly, "I'm fond of Matt. Not as fond of him as you, perhaps, but if he hasn't the nerve for it, I'll see that nobody reproaches him. Not even the newest roustabout."

"It's awful to stand here and hope he doesn't do it. Oh, I hate the whole business," she cried. "I'm sorry I ever heard of carnivals. As for being a good trooper I can't help wondering what difference it's going to make to the world, Matt's doing this. What does it solve? All it does is give a few hundred people a moment's thrill."

"Oh, but what a thrill," said Slim, smiling. "You know, kid, there aren't many men left in this world that aren't afraid. You know what I mean? We're all of us soft. We grow afraid of death, we're afraid of tripping over a milk bottle and breaking our necks, we get scared of going broke, of losing our health, of loving somebody too much. We're all of us ruled by our fears. It didn't used to be that way." He said reverently," and then some guy comes along who's not afraid of anything. He's not scared of standing up and risking his fool neck, and what's more he doesn't risk it for money, he just risk it for the thrill of risking it. You know what I mean?"

"It gives people a kind of courage just to watch him. It's like he was looking death right in the eye and saying, who's afraid? What's all the fuss about?"

He stopped and gave her a rakish smile. "Forget it," he said. "I'm just a frustrated old carny man. I envy Matt, I envy him his nerve. I wouldn't dare think of such a thing. Nobody else would, either, not that I know of."

Capri squeezed his arm gratefully. "You're nice, Slim. Thanks."

"Thanks for nothing."

"What time is it now?"

"Eleven-forty-five."

She nodded. "I guess I'll go and see Matt," she said.

Capri walked along the midway, keeping her eyes averted, not looking up least she see the dizzyingly high tower that in fifteen minutes would be laced with spotlights. She walked numbly under its shadow and entered the little tent at its base.

"Well, look who's here," said Ma Boone. "I'm just puttin' a little makeup on the lad."

"Makeup!" said Capri, startled.

"Hello, Capri," Matt said. She raised her eyes and looked at him steadily. He was feverishly excited; his eyes burned into hers. She found that she had to look away.

"He looks very handsome," said Mr. Gayfeather from the corner. "Quite a set of muscles."

"Well, it's no cinch to be an acrobat," Capri heard herself saying with a touch of lightness.

Someone stuck their head inside the tent, and said, "We're putting on the spotlights now, Matt. You be ready in ten minutes."

No, thought Capri, no. He mustn't do this.

"You still planning to go into this business, Capri?" asked Mr. Gayfeather with an ironic smile.

"How do I know?" she asked irritably.

"She's in it right now," said Matt calmly.

She looked at him scornfully, hating him. He was happy. This was his big night. He believed he was at last coming into his own. She wondered how she had ever tolerated such a friend, a boy who had no normal feelings at all, who enjoyed danger and could demand it.

I don't really know him at all. I don't want to. It isn't safe, she thought numbly.

"Okay, Matt," sang out Doc. "It's midnight, and Slim's beginning his spiel over the amplifier."

"Right. Thanks, Doc."

"Good luck, boy," said Ma, and kissed him jauntily on his cheek.

"Thanks, Ma." He put his arm around her and held her tight for a moment. "And Capri -—"

"Yes," she said stiffly. "Good luck, Matt."

He leaned down and kissed her quickly on the lips. That was when she first learned that Matt, too, was afraid. She could feel it in the trembling of his arm. "Good luck," she whispered again.

He walked out without looking back, the spangles on his white trunks glittering orange in the light.

"Ladies and gentlemen," cried Slim at top speed, his voice loud with excitement that was not entirely simulated, "tonight we have for you a death-defying dive -—"

Capri found a position between her mother and Mr. Gayfeather.

"Do you think you'll go through with it?" asked Francia. "Josh, do you?"

"I don't know," said Mr. Gayfeather, "but give me your hand, my dear. With all this suspense I need something to hold fast to."

I have nobody, thought Capri. I have nothing.

The platform was menacingly high; the spotlights played across it mercilessly, then dipped to find Matt as he climbed the rungs of the ladder slowly, surely, not once glancing down.

"Dear God," prayed Capri, "please make him turn around."

Up, up he climbed until the spangles on his trunks stopped flashing, until his face was only a blur.

"He's there now, folks. He's at the top. Another moment and -—"

Another moment and he'll turn around to come down, thought Capri. No one will mind.

There was growing among the crowd a sound like the wind blowing through a canyon. It was as though the whole crowd stirred at one time, restlessly, catching their breath as one person, holding it until Matt leaped.

"Francia," said Capri. "Francia!"

They would have to stop it immediately because, of course, it was apparent now that Matt planned to make the dive. She thought she might be ill. She wanted to scream something at Francia, but she could not open her mouth.

He was on his toes now, leaning forward. There was not a sound from the crowd. There was not even a sound from Capri. All the words she wanted to say were jammed in her throat.

He moved. He leaped. He dove. A thousand people screamed at once, and then there was silence, sheer, absolute silence. But Capri had closed her eyes.

Then Francia was throwing her arms around her. "He's safe, Capri," she was crying out. "Capri, listen to me. He's alright."

She opened her eyes, not believing. "Where?" she demanded. But there he was, the spotlight gleaming across his wet chest. She could see him. He was safe. He had done it!

A terrifying happiness burst through Capri. A tremendous pride overwhelmed her. She moved forward with the crowd, loving where once she had hated, loving everyone she touched, everyone she saw.

"Matt," she cried.

He heard her. He turned and waved. As they grinned at one another before he plunged into the tent, she saw that all his fear had vanished, and realized that with them her own fears had gone, too. For she had endured it with him every step of the way. In a sense she, too, had jumped, if only in her heart.

With the glorious new vision Capri stared about her at the carnival, at the pinwheels of revolving light, at all the gaudy toys and thrills, her nostrils wide to the smell of sawdust and oil, and popcorn and peanuts and heat. Then, carefully, defiantly, she raised her eyes to the diving platform.

Tomorrow night, she thought, it won't be as bad, and the next night it may be even easier. And, perhaps, at last I'll not mind it at all. And then I'll have become a real trouper.

CHAPTER TWENTY-FOUR

There were sixteen candles on the enormous white cake, and in the center Ma Boone had fashioned a magician's wand from a licorice stick. It was one o'clock in the morning. The last of the Saturday night crowd had vanished and the midway was empty. They were all in the Bingo tent, which once had brought them such catastrophe, but now came close to bursting as everyone crowded in to wish Capri a happy birthday.

She had been allowed, this once, to see the carnival's close. She had been allowed, too, as a gift from Professor Archie, to wear Molly spangles for an hour and help him on the platform with the disappearing eggs and the reappearing white rabbits. She had ridden on the Ferris wheel with slim, and pitch pennies with Doc. She had never had a lovelier birthday.

"Many happy returns," said Ma.

"I've never seen a more beautiful cake," vowed Capri.

There was a four-leaf clover mounted and framed as a gift from Ma. Slim had fashioned for her a complete set of magician's boxes, with clever false bottoms and vanishing doors. Mr. Gayfeather had sent a scrapbook made of fine imported leather. And from Matt, who could afford such gifts now that his act has been featured in *Billboard*, there were heavy gold bracelets such as he knew Francia used to wear on the stage.

But from Francia came the most wonderful present of all -—a worn black cape with a scarlet satin lining.

"Fran," cried Capri. "Is it -—?"

Across the candles Francia smiled. "Yes," she said. "It was your father's."

"Major Marvel's own cape!" said Archie with awe. They all gathered close to touch it. When they had done so, they regarded Capri with the reverent respect that only show people can evince for the daughter of a champion.

"She'll grow to it fine," said Archie. "From the start her fingers were full of magic."

For a moment Francia's eyes were full of sadness, then pride overcame her. "Here, here," she said crisply, "our budding young magician must cut her cake."

Capri laughingly accepted the steak knife that Charlie Marconi offered her.

"Now you must make a wish," said Ma Boone. "A fine, sturdy wish."

Capri looked into the faces that shone faintly from the light of candles. River Junction lay far behind them now. It was difficult to remember just where they were, the towns came

199

and went so quickly, but it had been Tuttling Mills last week and tomorrow it would be Victory Corners. Tonight, after the party, the roustabouts would again swarm over the midway like locusts to bring the towering amusement structures to earth and reduce the tents to so many piles of baggage. The trucks would drive close to swallow their burdens until presently there would remain only a few rubbish fires to show the boundary lines of what had once been a carnival of gaiety. And as the sky brightened in the east the crimson trucks and trailers would begin to move, each person carrying with them a chain of memories that ran together like ink on a wet page, for they were carny folks with gypsy in their blood and a rainbow around the next corner.

"Have you made your wish?" asked Doc.

Capri shook her head. For what was there left to wish? She had never before felt so alive or free. She had grown up the first night Matt had made his leap. Now she knew that there was no security in the world such as Francia had wanted for her -—there was only a curious necessity to follow one's own heart and find one's own purpose, as Matt had done and Francia, too, in her own way.

She might make a wish for Francia, but there was no need, for when the season closed Francia and Mr. Gayfeather were going to be married and live a quiet winter at the farm until March brought the return of the carnival. For Francia it would be the rounding of a circle.

As for herself there were many things for which she might wish, but there were none of them that she did not already grasp or could touch by the reaching.

CARNIVAL GYPSY

She smiled at Matt. "I have nothing left to wish for," she said, and bent to her task of cutting the cake.

THE END

ABOUT THE AUTHOR

Dorothy Gilman Butters – 1923 to 2012

Dorothy Edith Gilman Butters started writing when she was 9. At 11, she competed against 10 to 16-year-olds in a story contest and won first place. Dorothy worked as an art teacher and telephone operator before becoming an author. She wrote children's stories for more than ten years and then began writing adult novels about Mrs. Pollifax–a retired grandmother who becomes a CIA agent. While her stories nourish people's thirst for adventure and mystery, Dorothy knows about nourishing the body as well. She used to live on a farm in Nova Scotia, where she grew medicinal herbs. Her knowledge of herbs comes through in many of her stories.

CARNIVAL GYPSY

Ms. Gilman did not get a chance to participate in today's technology. Every book or short story she ever wrote was handwritten and/or typed on a typewriter. To introduce this author to newer generations of readers her family is in the process of converting all of her first stories into digital format for re-publishing in paperback, hardback, eBook and audio formats.

BOOKS BY THE AUTHOR –
REPUBLISHING IN 2023

ENCHANTED CARAVAN – Originally Published in 1949 – Republished 2023

CARNIVAL GYPSY – Originally Published in 1950 – Republished 2023

RAGAMUFFIN ALLEY – Originally Published in 1951

THE CALICO YEAR – Originally Published in 1953

FOUR PARTY LINE – Originally Published in 1954

PAPA DOLPHIN'S TABLE – Originally Published in 1955

GIRL IN BUCKSKIN – Originally Published in 1956

HEARTBREAK STREET – Originally Published in 1958

WITCH'S SILVER – Originally Published in 1959

MASQUERADE (republished under Heart's design) – Originally Published in 1961

HEART'S DESIGN – Originally Published in 1963

TEN LEAGUES TO BOSTON TOWN – Originally Published in 1963

THE BELLS OF FREEDOM – Originally Published in 1963

THE MAZE IN THE HEART OF THE CASTLE – Originally Published in 1983

NEWER BOOKS AVAILABLE TODAY IN PAPERBACK AND EBOOK FORMAT

UNCERTAIN VOYAGE – Originally Published1967

CLAIRVOYANT COUNTESS – Originally Published 1975

A NUN IN THE CLOSET – Originally Published 1975

A NEW KIND OF COUNTRY – Originally Published 1978

THE TIGHTROPE WALKER – Originally Published 1979

INCIDENT AT BADAMYA – Originally Published 1989

CARAVAN – Originally Published 1992

THALE'S FOLLY – Originally Published 1999

KALEIDOSCOPE – Originally Published 2002

MRS POLLIFAX SERIES

THE UNEXPECTED MRS. POLLIFAX – Originally Published 1966

THE AMAZING MRS. POLLIFAX – Originally Published 1970

THE ELUSIVE MRS. POLLIFAX – Originally Published 1971

A PALM FOR MRS. POLLIFAX – Originally Published 1973

MRS. POLLIFAX ON SAFARI - Originally Published 1977

MRS. POLLIFAX ON CHINA STATION – Originally Published 1983

MRS. POLLIFAX AND THE HONG KONG BUDDHA – Originally Published 1985

MRS. POLLIFAX AND THE GOLDEN TRIANGLE -Originally Published 1988

MRS. POLLIFAX AND THE WHIRLING DERVISH – Originally Published 1990

MRS. POLLIFAX AND THE SECOND THIEF – Originally Published 1993

MRS. POLLIFAX PURSUED – Originally Published 1995

MRS. POLLIFAX AND THE LION KILLER – Originally Published 1996

MRS. POLLIFAX INNOCENT TOURIST – Originally Published 1997

MRS. POLLIFAX UNVEILED – Originally Published 2000

BONUS MATERIALS FOR THE READERS

Central New Jersey Home News, page 14, Thursday, May 17, 1944

Miss Dorothy Gilman, daughter of Dr. and Mrs. J. Bruce Gilman of 53 Cleveland Avenue, Highland Park, a student in painting at the Pennsylvania Academy of Fine Arts, Philadelphia, will compete for a $1,100 Cresson Traveling Scholarship.

Central New Jersey Home News, page 15, Friday, May 19, 1944

Girl Competes for Travel Prize

Miss Dorothy Gilman, Student in Painting Tries for Scholarship

Miss Dorothy Gilman, daughter of the Rev. and Mrs. J. Bruce Gilman of 255 Handy Street, a student in painting at the Pennsylvania Academy of the Fine Arts, Philadelphia, is competing this week for a $1,100 Cresson Traveling Scholarship, according to an announcement from Joseph T. Fraser, Jr. secretary of the academy.

The award, $900 of which must be used for foreign travel, and the remaining $200 for tuition at the academy next year, was founded in 1903 under the terms of the wills of Emlen Cresson and Priscilla P. Cresson, as a memorial for their son, William Emlen Cresson, Academician. These annual awards were originally intended to provide a summer of travel and study in Europe for outstanding art students. Because of the war, the Orphans' Court of Philadelphia has decreed that the scholarship might be given for travel "In the Western Hemisphere."

Central New Jersey Home News, Page 13, Thursday, May 25, 1944

Dorothy Gilman Wins Award

Miss Dorothy Gilman, daughter of Dr. and Mrs. J. Bruce Gilman of 255 Handy Street, has been awarded a Cresson Memorial scholarship of $1,100 for further study of painting.

The scholarship is given to students of the Pennsylvania Academy of Fine Arts, Philadelphia. Nine hundred dollars must be used for traveling and $200 for tuition, according to the grant founded in 1903. Formerly the award was used for summer study in Europe, since the war travel in the Western Hemisphere is permitted.

Central New Jersey Home News, page 6, Thursday, September 17, 1945

Dorothy Gilman Becomes Bride Weds Edgar A. Butters Jr. At Cheshire, Father Officiates

Dr. and Mrs. J. Bruce Gilman of Highland Park, who are at their summer home in Massachusetts, announce the marriage of their daughter, Miss Dorothy Edith Gilman to Edgar Adamson Butters, Jr, son of Mr. and Mrs. Edgar A. Butters of Milltown.

The wedding was held on Saturday morning in the First Baptist Church of Cheshire, Mass. Dr. Gilman performed the ceremony, assisted by the Rev. Chandler Holmes. Only the Immediate families attended.

Mrs. Butters is a student at the Pennsylvania Academy of Fine Arts, and an instructor in art at the Graphic Sketch Club of Philadelphia.

Mr. Butters, a graduate of Rutgers, 1938, has Just received his honorable discharge from the Army. He was inducted in May 1941, served overseas for 36 months with the Signal Corps and holds the Bronze Star Medal and five campaign stars.

Mr. and Mrs. Butters will make their home In Philadelphia, where Mr. Butters will do graduate work at the University of Pennsylvania.

DOROTHY GILMAN BUTTERS

Central New Jersey Home News - page 8, Thursday, June 6, 1946

High School Alumni, Students, Veterans Join for Exhibition

Participants in the art exhibition by the Art Club and art department of New Brunswick Senior High School this week have been announced. Taking part are former students, current students, and veterans.

Dorothy Gilman Butters, illustrator, Moore Institute, Pennsylvania Academy of Fine Arts, who won a Cresson $1,000 scholarship and a $100 Toppan prize.

Nick Maltese, who recently held a one man show in New York and has sold a picture to the Art Students League. Others are, Frank Suto, Art Career School, Bradley University; Bruce MacPhail, cartoonist, American School of Design; Bill Giacalone, Art Students' League; Jack Johnson, Art Career School, Ruth Garretson, and Alice Goldt, Parsons' Art School; Claire Gladstone and Louis Szendrey, Newark Art School; Willard Gordon, display artist: designer and maker of silk screen posters; Ray Boegen; George Schmidt, who studied at Rutgers and the University of Pennsylvania and who will teach art at Pennsylvania.

Students whose work was exhibited at the Scholastic Art Exhibitions are Doris Yetman, Lucy Ciancia, Joyce Lashe, Vivian Balis, Marianna Szasz, Edward Bradley, Richard Warn, Margaret Noe.

Visitors are welcome.

CARNIVAL GYPSY

The Berkshire Eagle, Pittsfield, Massachusetts - Tuesday, Page 9, November 15, 1949

Author Here For Book Week Observance

Mrs. Dorothy Rutters To Re at Library and Women's Club

To feature the observance of National Book Week locally, Mrs. Dorothy Gilman Butters, author, and daughter of a former minister in Pittsfield, will lead programs tomorrow at the Berkshire Athenaeum and the Women's Club.

Mrs. Butters is the author of The Enchanted Caravan, a teenage novel published in March of this year. She is the daughter of Rev. and Mrs. J. Bruce Gilman who are now summer residents of Pontoosuc Lake. Mr. Gilman was pastor of the Morningside Baptist Church from 1903 until 1919.

Tomorrow afternoon Mrs. Butters will be the guest at a party at the local library given by the Junior Friends of the Athenaeum. This will also be the first meeting this winter of the Junior Friends, and boys and girls of high school age are invited to attend and join the group.

In the evening Mrs. Butters will be the guest of the Women's Club Wednesday Evening Book Review Club at a dinner in the club building on Wendell Avenue at 6. A discussion will follow at 6.45.

Berkshire Athenaeum originally built in 1876 still stands today.

CARNIVAL GYPSY

Central New Jersey Home News - Page 23, Thursday, April 27, 1950

Dorothy Gilman Butters Has Second Juvenile Book on Sale

Dorothy Gilman Butters, daughter of the Rev. Dr. and Mrs. Bruce Gilman of Highland Park, has a second juvenile book on the market. "Carnival Gypsy" follows close on the heels of "Enchanted Caravan" whose first edition was completely sold out.

The new book is the story of Francia Abbot Maccomb and her daughter, Capri, who inherited a carnival at the death of Francia's brother.

The troubles they encountered at the hands of the manager, a shady character who hoped by discouraging the pair to get control of the traveling band, their efforts to clean up gambling tents and replace them with legitimate entertainment is only part of the story.

The characterization of circus performers, mechanics and roustabouts is well done and the romantic interlude that appeals to the teen ager reader is gracefully and tactfully accomplished. Mrs. Butters seems to have a real knowledge of carnival jargon, troupers and practices and even explains some of the tricks of the trade. If you've always wanted to know how a woman is sawed in half, you can find the answer in "Carnival Gypsy".

The author won her first literary prize in a short story contest sponsored by The Sunday Times when she was only 11 years old. *Later, she decided to become an illustrator, went to the Academy of Fine Arts for six years and won a Cresson Traveling Scholarship to Europe in 1943.*

Mrs. Butters and her husband, a veteran and a history teacher, live in Morris Plains.

The Berkshire Eagle, Pittsfield, Massachusetts, Page 11, Saturday, April 29, 1950

Lanesboro Given Credit for Novel Background

The carnivals in Lanesboro were the inspiration for the latest teen age novel by Dorothy Gilman Butters, daughter of a former Pittsfield 'minister.

The story, titled Carnival Gypsy, has been published by MacRae Smith.

Mrs. Butters is the daughter of Rev. and Mrs. J. Bruce Gilman and now lives in Morris Plains, N.J., with her husband. Her father was pastor of the Morningside Baptist Church here from 1903 until 1919.

The book is Mrs. Butters" second teen-age novel, The first, "Enchanted Caravan", was published last year and received favorable reviews across the country.

"Carnival Gypsy" is the story of a woman who inherits a traveling carnival and, with her 15-year-old son, *(this should be daughter)* decides to take over running the show, much to the consternation of the manager.